POETS OF AFRICA

The Lianja Epic

POETS OF AFRICA

The Lianja Epic

Mubima Maneniang'

EAST AFRICAN EDUCATIONAL PUBLISHERS
Nairobi • Kampala • Dar es Salaam

Published by
East African Educational Publishers Ltd.
Brick Court, Mpaka Road/Woodvale Grove
Westlands
P.O. Box 45314, Nairobi

East African Educational Publishers Ltd.
Pioneer House, Jinja Road
P.O. Box 11542
Kampala

Ujuzi Educational Publishers Ltd.
P.O. Box 31647, Kijito-Nyama
Dar es Salaam

First published 1999

ISBN 9966-46-766-1

Printed in Kenya by Sunlitho Ltd., P.O. Box 13939, Nairobi, Kenya

Acknowledgements

I am very grateful to many individuals and organisations who have helped me to write *The Lianja Epic*. They are too many to be listed in full, but I mention the narrators, the dancers and singers who allowed me to witness their live performances of the epic and to interview them.

I owe gratitude to the libraries of the universities of Nairobi, Lagos and Ibadan, the University of Lagos, African Studies Department, the African American Institute in Washington D.C., the Mobutu Sese-Seko National Theatre of Zaire (now the Democratic Republic of Congo), as well as the National Educational Institute, Kinshasha.

I am thankful to Professor F.B. Akporobaro and Professor Abdulaziz of the University of Nairobi, and Mr Austin Bukenya of Kenyatta University. Without their generous help and expertise, this work would not have been completed.

Dedication

This book is dedicated to the Mubima family and
to all griots of the world who marvel at the beauty of oral art.

Introduction

The Lianja Epic is a long narrative poem that recounts the heroic deeds of a legendary descendant of the Mongo people of the Democratic Republic of Congo - DRC - (formerly Zaire) in Central Africa.

With the themes of peace, unity and reconciliation at its centre, the epic has been passed down orally from generation to generation since around the 14th century, and is still popular today in the DRC where it is performed in both the city and the country, and on radio and television. The Mobutu Sese-Seko National Theatre has also toured all over the world with their adaptation of *The Lianja Epic*.

The name of the Mongo who first narrated this epic is not known. Its composition has been gradual and collective, changing slightly from narrator to narrator and generation to generation, with variations among the different sub-tribes of the Mongo ethnic group. Suffice it to say that every performer or narrator of the epic can lay claim to its authorship.

Thus, Biongo of Nkolobeke, Mama Isaso of Bamania, Bonkundo of Kiri, Kanda of Mbandaka and five other performers who allowed me to record their live renditions of the Lianja epic between 1984 and 1985 are the "authors" of the text presented here. This final version is an amalgamation of what I considered to be the best from their various performances.

Before now, *The Lianja Epic* had never been published in either English or French. However, there is said to exist a Flemish edition in the archives of Belgium which would be out of reach of the majority of scholars of oral literature. Thus, the purpose of this book is to make available an English translation for wider readership.

Sadly, the greater part of the Congolese oral literature — the Luba love songs, the intermediary and personal poetry, the condensed and witty Mongo lyrics, the complex symbolism of Bakongo son-cycles and many others — remain almost unknown to most lovers of oral literature and those interested in exploring the wider ranges of poetic and narrative creativity. This state of affairs can be attributed to the biased educational systems which obtained during both the colonial period and after, and also to the cost of collecting oral materials and transcribing them and publishing them.

But the importance of *The Lianja Epic* does not reside only in the fact that it is a distinctive category of literary composition, but also in the aesthetic presentation of an experience that is both fascinating and profound. The epic expresses cultural and historical traditions, as well as deep thoughts. More importantly, the epic derives from the life of the people performing it; the socio-historical, economic and religious context in which they live. It is a heritage of artistic performance, cultural continuity and social values. It passes ideas from one generation to another while still reflecting development and changes in outlook between the different generations.

The epic is also an embodiment of group solidarity. People talk, meet, laugh, criticise, blame. It is a feast of music, dance and drama during which the participants gesticulate, shout, clap and ask questions. Though they might have participated in a performance of the epic several times before, when another one is staged, they flock over to attend it in order to acquire more knowledge.

Like most oral forms, the epic can be extended, transformed, readjusted to fit the realities of the society in which it is performed. This flexibility and adaptability is made possible in the epic because its performance is based on a loose elaboration of events. The central character sometimes has the characteristics of a culture bringer[1], which may not be the case with an historical or literary epic.

In contrast, the historical epic usually deals with the genealogies or the migrations of a particular people and thus requires a verbatim recitation. Although it may leave room for improvisation, the performer is limited since the recitation is "usually for occasions".[2] The Kuba Royal Epic and the Babemba and Baluba recitations about past migrations are such historical epics.

An epic poem or literary epic is also a narrative of some length which deals with events of a certain granduer and importance. Most of them are based on real-life occurrences such as wars. "The events and characters in this type of epic enhances the belief in the worth of human achievement, dignity and nobility of man".[3]

Some scholars have argued that once oral art forms are transcribed they can no longer be referred to as oral. The debate is on-going (and perhaps intractable), but in transcribing *The Lianja Epic* I have endeavoured as much as possible to retain its "oralness". Only essential and short notes are given to explain some passages in the text. More notes would have been required for a thorough comprehension, but this would have resulted in over-burdening the text with commentary, and hence an unnecessarily huge book and a loss of that oral feeling. I have also left out all material that seem to be a digression from the text in a bid to avoid a style unacceptable in the English language though acceptable in the original language.

The historical account has been given as accurately as possible with no changes in the sequence of events. However, I have tried my best to make the story around the hero more dramatic.

I have retained some words in the original language because I could not find the equivalent in English (which is my fourth or fifth language). Words like "kapokier" and "nsafu" (the former being a type of tree, while the latter refers to a fruit growing in a specific type of forest) have been retained as no terms could describe them correctly. Likewise, the term "Ngiambe" (which means God the

Almighty) has been retained because the Mongo belief regarding the name of the Creator is that it should not be tampered with; any attempt to do so may cause natural disasters in Mongoland.

Titles and sub-titles have been employed in the body of the epic text although oral poems usually do not employ this style. I have used it because *The Lianja Epic* now belongs to two genres of literature.

The reader will also note that some sentences have been cut regardless of the English grammatical rules. This is where the narrator might have paused to emphasise some very important points or gauge his audience's attention.

The Mongo People

Traditionally, oral literary forms were presented as mere texts without any contextual material. Today, however, it is recognised that oral poems and narratives, especially in written forms, require some understanding of the social, cultural, historical, geographical and anthropological context in which they are set.

The Mongo people of the Democratic Republic of Congo emanate from Bantu stock. Their population is estimated at more than five million. Although they belong to the same ethnic group, they are divided into many different sub-groups, each speaking a different dialect. In fact, there are so many cultural differences among the Mongo that sometimes it is difficult to consider them as one people. Because of their number, the Mongo are well-known and wield great economic and political importance within the Democratic Republic of Congo.

Mongoland occupies the greater part of Congo's equatorial forest, the home of many animal species interspesed with many rivers, lakes and streams with varieties of fish. The soil is very fertile and the material culture of the people is diverse.

Occupation and culture

Traditionally, the Mongo have lived on agriculture. It is the rhythm of the seasons which determines which cash or food crops to grow and hence the pattern of the Mongo way of life. The rainy season lasts nine months, from mid-August to mid-May, while the dry season lasts only three months. During the dry months (when the fields are being prepared for the next season), hunting and fishing are the major occupations. Mongo men and women cover long distances and stay away from their families for weeks or months, selling dry fish or meat from village to village or town to town. The dry season is also a time for visiting and for social functions like marriages and other cultural and religious ceremonies.

Potatoes, maize, yam, vegetables, roasted meat or fish served with various sauces constitute the basic food. The evening meal is the main meal of the day.

Although the Mongo are not herdsmen, each family keeps some cows, goats or poultry. The Mongo are not professional iron-workers or potters, but they make iron hoe blades, spearheads and clay pots for sale and for their own use. The presence of metal has greatly improved fishing, hunting and agriculture, making the people more materially dependent on these activities.

Mongo also make traditional weapons and digging sticks. In the area inhabited by the Tetela, metal, raffia and wood are used extensively for personal adornment as well as for tool-making, and are considered a necessity. Clothes of all designs are made of raffia, especially for traditional chiefs and their families. The skins of some animals, such as lions and leopards, are used to make clothing for traditional ceremonies, while those of goats and sheep are used to make drums, shoes, mats, etc.

Poles and mud are used to build huts, which are rectangular in shape with long, thatched roofs. The furniture for these huts typically includes a small table made of wood, some chairs roughly made of sticks or wood, cooking pots and water pots, gourds of different shapes and sizes, fish traps and baskets which are hung against the wall, fishing nets, woven baskets, and beds made of bamboo or wood. The men keep their fishing and hunting spears under their beds where their wives or daughters cannot touch them because it is believed women can diminish the luck of a hunter or a fisherman.

Religion

The Mongo people believe in one God, whom they call *Ngiambe*, the Supreme Being who created heaven and earth and lives alone in his cosmos. He cannot be seen; neither can He be reached directly by human beings. It is the *Bilima* (the Spirits) and *Bankolo* (the Ancestors) who act as intermediaries between *Ngiambe* and human beings.

The common belief is that the Spirits and the Ancestors live among human beings and protect them against the evil spirits who would harm them. The *Bilima* *(Elima)* are capable of possessing human beings and using them from time to time to fulfil their own wishes or those of *Ngiambe*.

Certain human qualities are attributed to the *Bilima*. They can be of either sex, they marry, they have children and they live in their world with their families. They have conflicts and quarrels, and they have friends and enemies. But there are also evil *Bilima* who can cause blindness, headaches, stomach-aches, nausea, fainting, lockjaw, whooping cough, skin disease, excessive sweating, madness, chronic anxiety, bad luck and even death. The evil spirits can also afflict women with painful periods four or five times a month, miscarriages, barrenness, and can cause a high rate of infant mortality. In fact, the Mongo believe that almost every disease is caused by bad *Bilima*.

Cosmology

Mongo cosmology comprises a rich reservoir for the narrative, an extensive universe filled with ancestors, good spirits, evil spirits, human beings, fabulous creatures, birds, animals, fish, hills, mountains, rivers, forests, valleys and lakes, all under the control of *Ngiambe*.

The common belief is that everything in the universe is controlled by specific forces. That is why there are good and bad spirits, water spirits, forest spirits, valley, mountain and bush spirits. The good spirits, or *bilima*, are permanently present. They are the symbolic personifications of the forces governing the flow of life. Consequently, the cosmogonic cycle is eternal, it repeats itself and death is seen simply as a transformation.

The Mongo cosmogony is composed of four cosmos. The first is the under-earth cosmos where the chief of evil spirits and all his followers resides. It is a malevolent world, populated by beasts and other evil forces that live in water, fire or air—causing earthquakes, drought, tornadoes, floods and fires. It is characterised by emptiness and darkness, suffering and misery; a world which has no contact with the higher cosmos and whose long-legged inhabitants have tails like crocodiles and walk around naked.

The second, or the earth cosmos, is inhabited by human beings It is a world of emotion and passion, dominated by hatred, anger, jealousy and revenge; a world of guilty people who fear death, anticipating it as a punishment for all their wrong-doing.

The third cosmos comprises the ancestors and the spirits where they have permanent interaction with the living.

The fourth and highest cosmos is divided into two; *Ngiambe* lives alone in the higher part of the cosmos while some select spirits who serve him reside in the lower part. He uses them or those in the third cosmos when He desires to communicate with the living.

It is believed that those Mongo who live a good life and respect the code of conduct of their society on earth will join the ancestors and the spirits in the third cosmos. Those who disobey society or Ngiambe will, upon their death, descend to the under-earth cosmos of the evil spirits, where they will remain, forever wretched.

Concept of time

Among the Mongo, as in many black African cultures, the question of absolute time is almost entirely absent. Time does not exist in a vacuum; it is not precise, absolute and measurable. Time is associated with important events or experiences in the society's everyday life.

As Professor John Mbiti has asserted, African people understand time in terms of events which have happened, those which are taking place and those which are about to happen.[4] Western people, on the other hand, place a high premium on consciousness of clock time because their temporal orientation stresses the preciousness and exactitude of time. When the narrator says that the hero, Lianja, was born after 200 years in his mother's womb (or any number of years in other versions of the epic), she or he is not strictly quantifying the time into seconds, minutes, hours, days or weeks, but merely indicating the importance of this particular event among the Mongo.

The Mongo temporal experience, it seems, more than any other aspect of their existence, is all pervasive, ultimate, immediate. Life, death and time are combined in a dialectical unit which is difficult to comprehend but which is symbolic in Mongo culture and religion.

Time in Mongo culture seems to be the reference point of all knowledge, experience and mode of expression. No other properties or realities such as space seem to be pertinent to the basic concerns of the Mongo as does the idea of time. All the realities and experiences in the epic are significant and symbolic, even if the method of dealing with the time during which they happen is not precise or objective and measurable.

Traditional medicine

Any discussion of Mongo traditional medicine of necessity involves a description of the *nganga kisi* (herbalist) and the *ndoki* (sorcerer). Their activities are related to the different ways in which both invoke good or evil *elima*.

Becoming a herbalist involves a thorough knowledge of the use of herbs, roots and plants, and using that knowledge for the benefit of the community in curing disease. The *nganga kisi* is a bridge between the sick person and the good spirits and, before treating his patient, he or she begins by invoking them for help. When the spirits enter him, he or she begins to speak in tongues, then diagnoses the sickness. Very often, if the patient is seriously ill, the *nganga kisi* goes into his "dark room" to consult with the spirits who advise on what roots or herbs to administer. Very ill people are kept in a special room within the *nganga kisi's* compound.

The *ndoki*, for their part, use evil spirits to harm people. They invoke, pray, make incantations, call the evil *elima*, burn fetishes, then direct the evil *elima* to do their evil bidding. Often, a *ndoki* acts on the request of one member of the community to bring harm to, or even kill another. At night, when people are normally asleep, they leave their houses and visit the graveyards where they cook and eat the flesh of their dead victims.

The Performance of the Lianja Epic

Always a public event, the traditional versions of "The Lianja Epic" are still performed among the Mongo sub-groups of Basengele, Bambole, Yomongo, Batetela and Basankus who occupy the area stretching from Lokolela through Basankus, Bumba, Mbandaka, Kisangani, Kindu and Lusambo to Kutu – an area about twice as large as the whole of France.

Although the epic is often performed for special ceremonies (for instance the Mobutu Sese-Seko National Theatre performed it on the occasion of Kenya's 20th Independence Anniversary) any member of the community can solicit a performance at any time. Generally, there is no specific narrator, but for public performances, story-tellers are hired and they are paid in food or palm wine.

The performance is an affair for the whole village and the telling is often done by women who pass the art on to their daughters. In the rural setting, the performances, which can go on for three to seven consecutive nights, start late in the evening after meals. Modern versions have been abridged to about 80 minutes to facilitate adaptation for radio, television or the stage.

The action progresses in three main streams: the narration (which is the most important), the dramatisation, and the singing (which is accompanied by horns, bells, xylophones and drums). At the beginning of the performance, the story-teller usually employs narrative methods in order to tune up his vocal and mental abilities, to warm up his audience and gain their confidence, and to establish a rapport with the supporting singers and musicians.

Beside the story-teller sit one or two young men or women. These are apprentices who will replace the story-teller when she or he dies. The apprentice confers time to time with the narrator on the sequence of episodes, inspires him or her when the thread of narration is lost, maintains discipline among the crowds and starts up refrains that are taken up by the audience as the raconteur warms up to his subject.

As the narrative progresses, it becomes richer with the teller incorporating many literary techniques (prosaic, poetic and dramatic) such as symbolism, tales, riddles, monologue, proverbs, mimicry and songs to keep the audience enthralled.

After a few episodes, there is a break of about half an hour during which time people assemble according to their age groups. The young boys and girls might spend the break dancing. They form a circle; a girl points at a boy of her choice and they meet in the middle of the circle and dance; they are cheered on by the rest of the group. The older people might prefer to go to their houses during the pauses to take food or kola nuts. Some stay at the arena and share palm wine with friends and relatives. A whistle is blown to signify the end of the break.

For the griot, the performances are an opportunity to exhibit acting and narrative talents, but they are also a spiritual experience. It is believed that the performance of the epic is a special task from the ancestors and that while a story-teller is performing, she or he is inspired and becomes an intermediary between the spirit world and the living. If a story-teller performs well, he or she acquires strength, health and courage. The songs, chants, monologues, mimics, praise-songs and eulogies constitute an address to *Ngiambe*, the spirits and the ancestors.

To announce the end of the performance, usually in the wee hours of the morning, the bard says: "Our Ancestral Forefathers never put end to the narration of this, neither shall we today."

Notes

1. D. Biebuycky, *The Epic as a Genre in Congo Oral Literature* (Nairobi: University of Nairobi, n.d.), p. 3
2. *Ibid.*, p. 3
3. *Ibid.*, p. 3
4. J.S. Mbiti, *African Religions and Philosophy* (Nairobi: East African Educational Publishers, 1969).

FIRST NIGHT

The Spirit Appears

The day the voice was heard
Silence surged into our cosmos like a star
That day the Mongo earth was shaken uncontrollably
A voice, round, powerful and mysterious
5   Opened and jolted our universe
Earth and heaven shuddered
The holy mountains of Mongoland were torn apart
The valleys of our cosmos burst into two that day
The voice opened the eyes of mankind
10   It lumbered among the hills and shook the thick Mongo forests
Making the birds fly timidly, animals crawl in desperation
And waters of the pools and rivers beat our shores without life
High crooked mountains of cloud descended upon our planet
And night settled down in the Mongo valleys, mountains and forests
15   It triumphed and killed the day
By thrusting the swords of darkness in the moon and stars
Mankind and all the aquatic creatures trembled
The beasts roared to thunder out their cries for fear of death
The monkeys on the trees, and birds in the darkness stared in terror
20   Ngiambe[1], the Creator, who moulded heaven and earth
Wondered why there was such commotion in mankind's cosmos?
He tore off the garments of the darkness and watched
He spat flames and coughed great jets of light
That scattered over the land of Waku-Waku[2]
25   A voice was heard from the sacred mountain of Bilima[3]
A Spirit whose body was light and whose head was human
Spoke thus: "I am Iania Anzaka Nzaka Bokulu Tondi[4]
I am the Spirit of the Forefathers sent to tell you
That you will see their bountiful gifts by the brightness of moon
30   That you will see the fulfilment of their tasks
That they will continue to bind all living things
As you know, the Forefathers are incomplete without Ngiambe's creatures
They want to express the might and ultimate power of Ngiambe
Who controls all His creatures with knowledge
35   Whose intelligence baffles the high councils of our Forefathers
When He speaks, mankind, Forefathers, Spirits and Gods listen."
So forcefully did the spirit speak, that the Mongo people began to trust him
Three men, led by Waku-Waku, went near him

1

Waku-Waku spoke with vehemence in these terms:
40 "This land belongs to the Mongo people,
We did not steal it from anybody but inherited it from our Forefathers
So that the Mongo people may populate it with wisdom and wealth
The forests yield to the stampede of beasts, animals and birds
The overflowing rivers, lakes, swamps and pools swell with fish
45 Yet in all this, we the heirs should have control
You, good Spirit sent by the Ancestors to deliver a message to their children,
Grant us peace, strength and good harvest."
As Waku-Waku spoke, the Spirit listened attentively
Then suddenly, he turned into a whirlwind
50 Which blew for a while and then stopped
A woman who was known for her wisdom went around the village crying:
"Men, women, how can we interpret such a great mystery?
We all must meet under the tree of wisdom
And find the truth behind the Spirit's message."
55 Yet no man, no woman dared show interest or enthusiasm
For commentary on a Spirit's message is forbidden
Among the dwellers of the earth cosmos
The wise woman went on: "Great Mongo warriors,
You are always overwhelmed with our Ancestors' powers,
60 Do not let the fire brought by the Spirit disappear and take away
The beautiful things *Ngiambe* has done for his creatures
Come out of your houses, let us open together our thoughts
We all know the Spirit's message unfolds eternal wisdom
From our meeting, all truth and resolutions will evolve."
65 The diviners came first, followed by the village counsellors,
Then the other people of Mongo
When the whole congregation was finally assembled,
The wise woman stood up and said:
"We all have heard the Spirit's skilful tongue
70 Revealing the truth of our existence
Our duty, men and women, is to perpetuate our Forefathers' wisdom
I have a vision of our land consumed by their wrath
If we ignore their message of wisdom and truth
How wonderful it would be if we inherited their wisdom!
75 If we could sing the same anthem they sung
An anthem which made them very powerful,
Their ladies beautiful, and their children prosperous!
I know that before they sent Iania
Assemblies of the Ancestors must have met
80 From sunset to dawn to discuss their people's fate."

2

Waku-Waku silenced the wise woman's words:
"Do not frighten us with unknown truth,
No people are happy who are troubled because of too much truth
Or made to feel guilty for their ignorance and lack of wisdom."
85   But the wise woman continued to speak as if nothing had been said:
"I see a vision of Mongoland invaded by locusts and beasts
If we keep silent and remain indifferent to our Forefathers' message
One day, small nations shall rise
And they shall destroy the whole of Mongoland
90   I see crowds of enemies exchanging words and carrying
Glimmering shields, spears and poisonous arrows to attack us."
Once again, Waku-Waku tried to stop Mama Isaso[5]
But no sooner had he uttered the first word,
Than the Spirit appeared again in their midst,
95   He intervened and said:
"Those who trust in their own wisdom and believe in their own immortality
Shall be made ash and dust!"
The Spirit took handfuls of earth in his right and left hands and said:
"These are your Forefathers who lived happily here on earth
100   These are the Spirits who protect you and intercede for you
We all are here today to tread on them: Spirits and Ancestors
We all depend on *Ngiambe* the Invisible
Yet Mongoland will remain powerful
If you obey Him by following His teachings
105   For He is the giver and guardian of life,
The one who can open the gates of the mountains of wisdom."
Iania approached Mama Isaso[5] and said:
"Here is the great wise woman of your land
It is through her that your Forefathers and Spirits have spoken to you
110   Because she can envision the shapes of your cosmos
In which abound those who always symbolize the destruction of creation
And those eager to perpetuate the cycles of God's creation through humankind
Mongo generations to come will never forget these words
And those of Mama Isaso
115   They shall develop sound minds
Greening themselves upon the powers of wisdom
And reflection granted to them by the Spirits
Happiness and great joy will be brought to them by one son of this land
As a reward for their searching minds and obedience
120   That son will roam the Mongo earth to discover the great mysteries of mankind
That son shall go and win, tearing apart the gates of enmity among tribes

3

Those who do not praise peace and unity will be torn like trees by their roots
Their ecstasies will be no more than effusions of their own blood
He will redeem, unite mankind and lead it to the path of eternity."
125   Only silence reigned in the gathering of the living Mongo
They listened to the wise Spirit
But not many of them understood what he said
For the Spirit's words fell like rain in its abundance
And only a few wise elders and diviners understood the wise one's message
130   No sooner had the Spirit finished speaking than he waved to the gathering
And disappeared in a whirlwind blowing towards the mountains
Transported by the Mongo Spirits and Ancestors,
He went to appear in another region
Someone stood up to curse the Sau-Sau[6], the enemy of the Mongo
135   Eager to announce their defeat as anticipated by the Spirit
But Waku-Waku warned him:
"Do not curse the Sau-Sau for the Spirit has already laid the foundation
For our future relations and that of our sons with his words and deeds
Besides, the Spirit did not teach us hatred, but love and unity
140   Our children and the children of our children shall rule the other tribes
Whoever swears to be faithful and loyal to his Ancestors and Spirits
Must contend with opinions from his enemies and friends
Remove the seeds of hatred from the enemy's words
And implant his own words of wisdom and love in their minds,
145   Teaching them through word and deed, his own greatness
For whoever denies the right of life to his fellow man denies his own life
For the reality of *Ngiambe*'s creation rests upon His own creatures:
Those today and others who shall come tomorrow, are part of the truth here
The sight of the Invisible goes beyond the boundaries of eternity
150   What the Spirit sent by our Ancestors has spoken
Is a challenge to the very truth of our being
Whosoever does not agree with these wise words will end the course of life."
The congregation listened, struggling with the meaning of the words
From the assembly burst out choruses of praise dedicated to the Forefathers
155   To the Spirits and to *Ngiambe* Himself
Poems of excellence were heard from all mouths, giving praise to the Invisible
Men, women and children gathered according to age and gender
To sing and dance and glorify *Ngiambe*
There was a great feast on Waku-Waku's land
160   For many days, people ate and drank and pledged loyalty to the Forefathers
When the celebration was over, the gathering dispersed
But the Spirit continued to appear in Mongoland

Any time Iania Anzaka-Nzaka appeared, Waku-Waku beat a drum:
"Ting Ting Dung Ting Tung du du du ting ting."[7]
165 To inform neighbouring Mongo villages
Of the Spirit's appearance
Then a great chorus of praise would burst forth with the anthem of glory
Words of praise and thanksgiving would echo throughout Mongoland
From the assembly of Spirits and Ancestors in their cosmos
170 A burst of voices would descend
Blessing Mongoland and flashing balls of purification fire
And showers to cleanse them of their wickedness and sin
The living played in the rain, running around the tree of wisdom
As the water cleansed and purified them
175 Those who had never seen the Spirit had their own ideas about him
His height, weight, form and the colour of his skin
Some insisted that he had human form and nature
Others said he was like the wind but with great powers and wisdom
Those who had seen him confirmed that he was young, stout and powerful
180 With magical powers to appear and disappear
He was light in complexion with black hair and green eyes like the Mongo
In height, living people on the earth cosmos matched him
The Spirit continued to appear and many Mongo people saw him
They entrusted themselves to him,
185 Knowing it was a blessing to see him
Women and children sat at the crossways to beg for protection from him
While the elders invoked him for plentifulness in all the regions
Those Mongo who were burdened on their heads and shoulders with disgrace
Pleaded for better and longer lives
190 And the Spirit granted a home, wealth and health to anybody who appealed
With his words he built the Mongo people's strength for future generations
Waku-Waku travelled from region to region to pass the message:
"All our regions are the Spirits' and Forefathers' dwelling places
All their gates must open to welcome the Spirit they have sent us
195 Be happy, rejoice, for prosperity will favour our villages
We are made wealthy and prosperous by the one they chose for us
The long days of sorrow whose seeds were sprouting among us are over
These bitter seeds would have been a blade among generations to come
Our Forefathers said that sorrow is like a crocodile
200 Which lays eggs on the beach
Where our children go swimming
It kills them and breaks the smoothness of their lives
The bounty that has been brought into our houses

Will not be forgotten by ages to come
205 You shall never forget the violent pains we endured
When our respect and love were discarded
They abandoned us and even the wretched of the earth
And worthless evil spirits made fun of us
All the neighbouring tribes laughed at us when our wives and children
210 Were crawling and begging for food from them
I, the descendant of the mighty Mongo tribe,
I, the proud Mongo child who was born of the invisible warrior,
I heard the shameless and rude Sau-Sau mocking me with their choruses
I groaned with heart ache and shame at their violence,
215 But my sole comfort was my dignity and *Ngiambe's* promise
I knew that one day, the Spirits and our Forefathers would plead with *Ngiambe*
For all their Mongo sons and daughters
I knew that the powerless Sau-Sau who mocked me would one day shudder
Before the powerful sons and daughters of Biongo."[8]
220 He spoke and spoke and spoke as if he wanted to take revenge,
As if the Spirits and the Ancestors stood for the longstanding grudge
Against the Mongo's eternal enemies, the Sau-Sau
His mind was lost in the midst of remembered pain and humiliation
He looked up to the sky with a sigh, murmuring inaudible words,
225 Meanwhile, other clans and tribes sat restless in their villages
Their elders, diviners and witchdoctors seldom closed their eyes in sleep
Waiting for the appearance of the Spirit
Whenever they heard distant voices singing, they assembled
Their clansmen sang welcome hymns to draw the Spirit's attention
230 They danced until morning and chanted incantations
But the Spirit never appeared
During that period, only the Mongo were reputed
For their obedience and faith in *Ngiambe*
Who had sent them the Spirit of redemption
235 The other tribes requested Waku-Waku's audience
Because he knew the Spirits' and the Ancestors' secret of intercession
A word from him filled them with joy:
"Issue the great call to obedience to *Ngiambe's* teachings,
Summon all your tribesmen and women, old and young."
240 At these words, many tribes changed their behaviour but some did not
Those who boasted of witchcraft, magic, hatred and murder
The evil ones who could change themselves into beasts
And harm their fellow men
Those who dabbled in the power of night magic

245 Hunting for human victims to slaughter like wild animals
Those who brought terror and calamities within the tribes
Those ones did not change.

Ngiambe Blesses the Mongo

Darkness engulfed Mongoland and the neighbouring villages,
Black blankets of clouds opened their gates and rain fell for many moons[9]
250 Rain, rain, rain, everywhere there was rain
There were showers of blessing and abundance in Waku-Waku's village
The Mongo sowed the ground with new life
The Spirits and the Ancestors joined the Mongo in their celebration
Then together, they all sang the hymn binding the living with the Ancestors,
255 Calling the names of their Forefathers, one by one and their clans
The representatives of *Ngiambe* rose from their sacred dwelling
Riding across Mongoland to the West
Generation after generation of Forefathers came to the celebration
They narrated tales about their cosmos
260 And sang the eternal anthem of *Ngiambe's* power
Which broke the boundaries of all the cosmos
Again and again, they repeated the hymn
Which was soon taken over by the living, the Ancestors and the Spirits
All who were present that day
265 Sang hymns and anthems
How could they have kept silent before *Ngiambe's* wonder!
How wonderfully they could praise Him, all with one voice
Mongo pride was reborn and the wilderness echoed with thankfulness
The whole gathering turned to the West
270 The source of Mongo life where the relics of the Forefathers were treasured
And from where the Mongo language of secrets
Comes breezing up the minds of the troubadours and diviners
Ngiambe in His cosmos watched and admired His own creatures
The Mongo rivers, lakes and oceans burst open with new life
275 In the equatorial forest, animals roared and murmured with joy
And *Ngiambe* watched them planting more seeds of life in the earth
The gigantic forest grew jungles, savannahs and bushes
Howled with a great symphony of beautiful voices and bird song
Ngiambe made the cycle of life explode in all directions
280 The waters of earth opened their hearts to the sky
The mountains spread dim light of wisdom and health
Announcing the end of a malicious night

7

A vast gleam hovered between life and death
But the sun, the moon and the stars had not been invited
285 The Ancestors and the Spirits were careful, they began to peer into the sky
And insisted that the celestial and heavenly bodies also be present
The living sent an emissary to call them
To descend on earth and join the creatures in celebration
But the heavenly bodies were offended that they had not been invited earlier
290 It was the moon who spoke for them all to the emissary:
"How disgraceful that the living have treated us like rotten corpses
Does a great family ignore some of its children
Even if the latter are said to be fools?
The family stands firm to protect them
295 And strives to ensure the foolish ones learn the language of wisdom
And through time and patience,
They too come to wipe away their unwise scars
And replace them with thoughts of balm."
She spoke these words of bitterness as the sun and the stars listened
300 The sun summoned the messenger, ordering him:
"Go back to the people of earth,
Tell them that the heavenly clan
Has decided to afflict the earth with calamity and disaster
We shall generate terror in their minds,
305 Making them drink and eat from the powers of darkness and night
We shall cease their high-handedness
Nobody can ascertain with such eagerness what future belongs to him
Only those who remain faithful to their truth succeed in their endeavours
Mongo people on earth think they are conquerors
310 They break into dance and song while their neighbours weave plots with tears
Such was the fate of the Sau-Sau who are today wretched."
Yet despite the anger of the celestial bodies,
The celebration on earth continued for it was a day of joy
That would be told to future generations
315 It was Nkanda, the elder son of Mongo's greatest griot
Who led the singers in praise song,
Chanting the Mongo variations of perpetuating life:
"I sing to *Ngiambe* who moulded this earth
I sing to *Ngiambe* who created and gave life to mankind
320 I sing to *Ngiambe* who sent us abundant rains
From which, life in Mongoland will spread to other regions
The quietness of remotest forests shall hear the Mongo voice,
Waku-Waku's tribesmen shall penetrate with the truth of life

8

The deepest caves of mankind
25 By their determination to serve and obey *Ngiambe*,
    They shall reach the four extremes of the world
    Crossing arid lands with courage,
    And traversing fierce darkness in the wild lands without fear
    Enemy tribes such as the Sau-Sau shall fear us
30 We shall all go across forests and bushes as heroes
    Avoiding confrontation and war with the bandit clans
    We shall seek only peace, friendship and unity
    We know tomorrow is ours for the bounty is in our house."
    As Nkanda sang, incantated and chanted, those in the gathering
35 Brimmed with joy and excitement
    Their eyes overflowed with tears of joy
    Prince Bola's singers took over from Nkanda
    And continued the same tune
    Great numbers of guests filled the arena:
40 Mortal Mongo, Ancestors, *Ngiambe's* delegates, Spirits,
    Invitees from other tribes and nations
    Among whom were rulers, councillors, heroes,
    Lords, kings, queens, army generals
    And even representatives of the enemy tribe, the Sau-Sau
45 All, living and Spirits, were there
    Of the women guests could be seen the Honorable Mama Ewando,
    Mama Yomamu the Queen of the Botwa (Pygmies),
    The soothsayer of the Ekonda
    The Bolia wise woman and the Princess of Basengele arrived together
50 From the West, came the great lady of Ngombe
    She rose in a mighty array of colours,
    Attracting an ocean of curious and inquisitive eyes
    Suddenly, the great poet Koyambga heralded Prince Lokenio's approach
    The most invulnerable old medicine women Bowoto and Bolengo emerged,
55 Saluting and preening like peacocks,
    Their heads adorned with aluring feathers
    The medicine women were followed by the chiefs of clans,
    Mumakheta, Bongdonga and Bongwolanga
    Who sat down with Analengo, the Immortal Chief of Atetela
60 Prince Bola's singers sang, beating the Mongo ground with their feet
    It was Waku-Waku who gave the sign with his right hand,
    Slowly, the tune changed, it became slow and stopped smoothly
    A great silence reigned in the congregation
    As the crowd waited anxiously to hear from Waku-Waku

365   **He moved into the circle and started a prayer song**
That was soon taken up by the gathering:
"We are proud creatures who possess full life
From *Ngiambe*, the Great Creator
We thank you and need your presence for this accomplishment
370   We are boastful only of the little truth we know
When our souls and minds are boggled by our ignorance, we panic
Hence scores of mortals roam around the world
Trying to find the very truth of creation
When sometimes you allow calamities to hit us
375   And misery to tear us apart
And threaten the very essence of our lives, we wonder
We are disturbed and think that life has no meaning
That you have permitted the charm of life to cast endless hurricanes
On mankind with the only aim of deranging your creatures
380   We are horrified and we retreat, we go astray
But you know us, you know that we are weak, foolish
Though we sometimes lose the sanity of our minds,
You still cater for our needs and remain faithful to mankind
Great Creator, we need your blessing to summon up courage
385   We need a word from you for us not to despair,
We need your power to escape the dangers and snares on earth
However scaring they may be, we shall overcome them
And our minds will be reinforced
And renewed by the Spirit you have sent us."
390   Then the prayer song stopped
A great silence reigned again for a long time
Each one present meditating and cross-examining himself
Then the Immortal Atetela Chief stood up and begged the congregation
To lend him its ears,
395   He stood up and said: "I bow to you all, the scions from *Ngiambe's* cosmo
I bow to you eminent Spirits, Ancestors and Forefathers,
I salute you representatives of great and powerful tribes
In the name of the mortal and immortal Mongo,
I salute you distinguished fellow Mongos,
400   I salute all of you in the name of our brotherhood:
I speak as a true and humble servant of *Ngiambe*,
Of our Ancestors, Forefathers and those yet to be born in Mongoland
By gathering here today, we have expressed our gratitude to *Ngiambe*
Who sent us Iania, the Spirit,
405   To remind us of our bond with Him

We thank Him for the abundant rain
We thank Him for weeding out one by one the seeds of hatred
Among our tribes, clans and families
We thank Him for the emissaries from His own cosmos
) Who hurried on their way to come and celebrate with us
I bow again to them and ask the crowds to cheer them."
Thunders of applause echoed from the gathering
"I am not worthy to address this multitude of God's emissaries, Ancestors,
Forefathers and outstanding guests assembled here
5 I know I lack their wisdom and eloquence,
But I speak as the precursor of our many famed Mongo orators
I do so for it is my prerogative to bow to *Ngiambe* and His emissaries,
The Ancestors and Forefathers
I would like to put it to the Mongo people and future generations
0 That only for love of Mongoland has *Ngiambe* sent us rain in abundance
To extinguish the fire of misery
The whole of Mongoland has suffered great sadness
Death, disease, poverty, calamity and misery haunted it
The griots, dancers and musicians of this land had abandoned their songs of joy
5 Their dance and performance of Mongo heroic deeds
The food of our souls and the nourishment of our bodies
Were chopped by malicious spirits with a heavy, sharpened axe
We see the light now after a long period of suffering
It is only *Ngiambe* who has brought back to us happiness
0 Would Mongoland have become eternally a land of distress?
Fellow Mongo men and women, shall we forget that disobedience to *Ngiambe*,
Hatred, jealousy, murder, theft, wickedness and lamentation
Bring only misfortune and disaster?
Are we not here to make firm resolutions?
5 Did not our Forefathers and Ancestors
Show us the path of wisdom and prosperity?
Have you decided to break or keep up the bond with them?"
So great was the silence, it seemed the place had changed into a tomb
An emissary from the cosmos of *Ngiambe*, spoke after (Chief) Analengo
0 Seeing him, you would think he was God himself, full of might
His head full of wisdom, had never succumbed to any burden
The tunic he wore was decorated with different colours
Blending blue, white and green
He stood up with his shining eyes transfixed on the crowds
5 He was tall but slender, light of complexion with curly hair
As he stood, thunder and wind blew, lightning flashed in the forests,

11

The living on earth beat their drums and blew their trumpets,
Ngiambe sent His bluebird which descended
And posed on His emissary's right shoulder
450   The bird shrieked like a human being and sang a melody
Its voice echoed across the Mongo sky, rivers, forests
And in the hearts of all those who could hear it in different cosmos
Even the Ancestors, Forefathers and Spirits cherished the heavenly bird
As it stopped singing, the emissary said:
455   "We have fulfilled the task *Ngiambe* had sent us to do,
But it will remain unfinished if you on this cosmos
Do not perpetuate it."
The few words he spoke were not easily understood by the mortals
Just as they did not understand the basic truth, of their own existence
460   It was now the turn of one Forefather to speak
All eyes were focused on him as he began
The living wondered what lessons he had to teach them:
"I thank all the skilful tongues which have spoken here
Above all, I thank *Ngiambe* who has assembled us here
465   Yes, *Ngiambe* implants His word through the Spirits
From time to time, He chooses one among them
And sends him to convey a message to the mortals
Spirits are gifted to tell the future of the living
When we see man weep because he is ruined by calamities,
470   Reduced to nothing by misery and poverty,
We know that the disastrous situation is caused by himself,
The mortal who once lived in happiness, wealth and dreams,
Set himself free from *Ngiambe's* teachings
He roams and roams again the whole earth in search of mysteries
475   Where his ambitions cannot bring him success
His imagination helps him achieve the unachievable
By tearing apart the great garments of truth, decency and honesty
Which bind the gates of infinity with humankind
What the mortal should always remember is that
480   Lucky is the one on whom *Ngiambe* shines His radiance,
For thenceforth he shall be given more years of plentifulness on earth
But he on whom *Ngiambe* shall not turn His friendly radiance,
An everlasting misery shall riddle him
So it was decided by Him, so it has been and shall be
485   Anytime the mortal keeps aloof from his own Creator,
Filling his soul with bitter grudges or unpleasant feeling,
He lays snares for himself

Never ever shall you Mongo men, women and children,
Violate the code of conduct we immortal beings passed to you
490 For whatever is possessed by humankind should be held
In trust for all future generations
Ngiambe knows, only you have the right to all things He created
Therefore, by your actions, never scandalize God's big human race
For you may break the natural bonds you have with Him
495 Our griots and soothsayers reveal to us that
Those Mongo who have been cursed because of misconduct,
Have ceased to be Mongo and have changed into beasts
Their wickedness has no bounds
They curse the upright Mongo
500 And plot against them
In anger, they send you their messengers
Threatening humankind through their many representatives on earth
But behold! remain imperturbed by them
For *Ngiambe* will always be with you
505 He will give you life's resources, unlimited,
That is why He, *Ngiambe,* has decided
That a boy full of knowledge
Will be among you
The wise and powerful young man will lead you to areas of plenty
510 He will show you abundant rivers, pools and lakes
That will leap over the white cliffs of Mongoland
And shoal of fish, crops and fruit that will overhang the Mongo earth
Such abundance will be enough for all the next generation."
After the Forefather had uttered these words,
515 He cleared his throat with water
Brought to him by another immortal, then sat down
The Forefather gave the Mongo nourishment for their existence
By his word he brought promise to their existence
He had honoured *Ngiambe* and the Spirits by announcing
520 The coming of Lianja in the midst of the Mongo people
Only he, a Forefather or a Spirit, could perform such a duty,
For only those immortals who have become closer to *Ngiambe,*
And have acquired the language for such occasions could do so
They know the words they must speak to the living and to *Ngiambe*
525 In the silence that reigned after the Forefather's long speech,
The mortal Mongo councillors urged Waku-Waku to speak
The wise and powerful Mongo raised himself from the crowds and said:
"Words have gone so deep into my heart and mind

Yet, I too, have been given the opportunity to speak,
530 Since past events give birth to new ones
I appreciate every word that has been said
Through their words, mine are fed by their wisdom
Yes, our life here on earth is hard,
But our persistence shall lead where our Forefathers and Ancestors are
535 Great honour is given to them: Spirits, Ancestors and *Ngiambe*
Who always rush to our aid whenever we find ourselves in trouble
I know that often the mortal collapses through his indulgence
I also know that only he who starts an epoch can have a vision of courage
Thus, I too, incite every mortal Mongo to greater courage
540 I uplift the Forefathers, the Spirits and *Ngiambe*."
Waku-Waku beat the drum and the celebrations continued until dawn
One by one, mortal and immortal returned home the following day

The End of Abundance in Mongoland

During those days of abundance all over Mongoland,
The enemy tribe, the Sau-Sau, was watching the Mongo people,
545 Monitoring their movements and detailing one by one, their secrets
The Sau-Sau knew it was important and useful to discover
The secrets of their enemy in order to destroy them easily
The Mongo people's meetings, gatherings and assemblies
Became haunted by hatred, jealousy and filthy words
550 Thoughts of murder, theft, disobedience to *Ngiambe*
Were openly manifested by the Mongo people:
Men, women and children, indeed the whole community
Was ravaged by thoughts of dissent and disunity
Children grew wild, lashed at their fathers and mothers
555 Incest, rape, murder, theft, hooliganism were rampant
Men divorced their wives, some married their own daughters
Others slept with their brothers' wives
Mothers cared neither for their children nor for their husbands
They kept themselves busy hunting for wealth using crooked means
560 A group of female evil spirits in their cosmos,
Watched the Mongo women's conduct with keen interest
They decided to send their representatives to live with the Mongo women
And teach them the most sophisticated methods of prostitution and adultery
The she-devils' duty was to teach prostitutes
565 How to chase after men and how to catch them
How to hunt them, haunt and woo them wherever they may be

In case of failure, which was rare,
The she-devils would attack the person and, in their anger,
They would send him deadly and horrible nightmares
570   During which the man would see a naked young woman
The most beautiful ever seen in Mongoland
This is the method Mongo women used
To create havoc in many families and among young men

Ngiambe Punishes the Mongo

Seeing the Mongo behave thus, *Ngiambe's* wrath grew
575   Their misconduct raged on, giving God no peace of mind
He decided to prepare His spirit for the last judgement
He said to Himself: "The triumph of the evil spirits will cease very soon
For I am going to make the Mongo stop their foolhardy behaviour
On earth, the Mongo people are still beleaguered by useless ambition
580   And hallucinations dictated to them by the evil spirits
Should I reduce the entire people to nothing or ash?
When the Mongo people were harassed by their enemy tribe, the Sau-Sau,
Decimated by famine, hunger, disease and earthquakes, I saved them
Do they think my wrath cannot destroy them?"
585   After *Ngiambe* had spoken like that to Himself
He called one of His wisest Spirits
And told him: "Hurry and go to the Spirits' cosmos,
Tell them to meet and send delegates to Mongoland
To inform the people that because of their madness
590   My punishment is forthcoming
Listen to me carefully:
After I had created man and placed him on earth
He was ignorant of life's meaning,
Uncaring of the bonds existing between him and I the Creator
595   This indifference brought a curse upon mankind
But I quickly changed that
I awoke new sense and gave new direction to mankind
Man became capable of differentiating bad from good
But among the many Spirits I myself created
600   Some have failed to understand the truth of their existence
That is why they wander through the universe and nag humankind
Look at them, they walk in circles with their emptiness,
Shocked by the hollowness of their existence
And the uselessness and meaningless of their life

605 They are infinitely asking themselves the meaning of their lives
As they are questioning themselves and pondering how to change their lives,
They are lost in their thoughts and thus go around all the cosmos
Creating havoc, death and misconduct among the living
Their target is to make mankind disappear with its cosmos
610 But you good Spirits are the precious gift I gave the living
As you vowed, you should always denounce the devil's folly
Help humankind to search for truth with their minds,
For truth is true if only it fertilizes the mind
By your help, human beings will be able to attain the power,
615 To choose between vanity and truth, wisdom and divine power
You, good Spirits, must teach them so that they acquire knowledge
Teach them how by the power of their knowledge
They can turn their empty thoughts into everlasting truths
Go now and see for yourself how the Mongo people are behaving."
620 As *Ngiambe* unravelled these truths,
The Spirit had nothing to say, for he could not comprehend
The behaviour of the living
He could not tell why the living had remained such ingrates
Despite all the wonders God had done for them!
625 Why should mankind surrender to evil spirits?
Whose duty is to harm, disunite and plant seeds of hatred!
Why cannot mankind understand that
If the evil spirits were truly as great as they claim,
They would not have been associated with evil
630 As the Spirit himself wrestled with many thoughts about mankind,
He left the cosmos of God, eager to help redeem the Mongo
When he reached the Spirits' cosmos, he made a call to assemble them
As the call to assemble the Forefathers and the Spirits was proclaimed,
All the inhabitants of the cosmos flocked in their greatest numbers
635 Individuals, families, clans and tribes of Forefathers and Spirits,
Proud to fill the meeting place, responded to the call by the messenger
Who wisely had prepared his speech and argument
The assembly of Spirits and Forefathers listened to him with wonder
They watched and observed, burning with a great desire to know
640 Why he spoke with impatience, forcing out his thoughts and words
As one with pent up emotions and difficult thoughts!
"Great and wise Spirits of *Ngiambe*, I salute you in the name of His power,
The One who is always with us and amongst us
All of you: man, woman, young and old, be blessed in His name
645 He is the One who moulded and designed our complex appearance,

Through millennia, He has perpetuated His creation in the universe
He has filled it with various species of plants, fish and animals
He has spread beautiful creatures all over
He has placed mankind over other creatures to control the earth
50 But how often does man get carried away by his own power
Generously given to him by *Ngiambe*, whom he now disobeys?
How many times has man been seen exercising his authority with cruelty
Spreading seeds of hatred among his fellow men?
I do understand the problems confronting mankind
55 And I therefore suggest that the devil
Who is always creating dissent on earth,
Be exiled into distant arid lands to die there,
For indeed, a mango tree whose sweet fruit grows in a wild forest
Feeds nobody on its juicy fruits
60 They fall to the ground to be eaten by wild animals and worms
So shall the devil's malice and intelligence be wasted
In the stony and arid lands where no human being lives
We must isolate man from the evil spirit to ensure his survival."
Scarcely had he finished speaking than the Forefathers
65 And other Spirits
Asked him to explain his ideas
It was a young-looking Spirit who said:
"No one in this assembly is able to grasp the words
That come from your mind and soul."
70 And the messenger immediately replied:
"I shall substantiate my thoughts and ideas
As long as I still have the floor to address this wise assembly
I am shocked and disturbed by a very serious threat made by *Ngiambe*
And try as I might to erase it from my mind, it emerges again and again
75 Everywhere I look, I see a vision of how *Ngiambe* is going to kill the Mongo
I see the Supreme Creator throwing the fire of His wrath upon the Mongo
The whole universe may perish because of the Mongo
Powerful and wise clans of Forefathers and Spirits,
I have come to reveal the secret intention of *Ngiambe*
80 In a very short period of time, *Ngiambe* will punish the Mongo
He will destroy them and all creatures living on their land
These are the few words I meant to say and we must hurry
I ask you to form a delegation which shall run to Mongoland
To implore all men and women to repent,
85 To change their conduct, which has become the subject of discussion
In all the cosmos created by *Ngiambe*."

The Queen Foremother stood up
And came into the middle of the circle
Cursing the devil and all his past and future generations
690   A lady of nobility, authority and respect,
She addressed the gathering with solemnity and seriousness,
Keeping her tone even:
"I greet you brothers and sisters here present and absent
The messenger Spirit has informed us of the destruction
695   The Mongo people are going to endure
For massive disobedience to *Ngiambe*
Right now, our preoccupation should be
How to reconcile *Ngiambe* and the Mongo people,
If they accept a reconciliation
700   Surely, *Ngiambe* will steer the Mongo back
Onto the path of redemption
Brothers and sisters, it should be the moral obligation of all of us
To help the Mongo repent and confess their sins
So they can reconcile with the Supreme Creator,
705   Only then, can we say we have performed our duty to *Ngiambe*,
And no immortal or mortal will be able to deny it
In planning the reconciliation and negotiation,
Our only aim and target shall be to make the Mongo people see
The beauty of God's words
710   I know people on Earth have their own thoughts
Different from ours,
But by the power of the Almighty and by our love for the living,
We can help them to have good thoughts
If you in this cosmos know this, let us be wise
715   And create for mankind an atmosphere of good deeds
Their continued disobedience to *Ngiambe* is also affecting our world
Ngiambe created us to help man improve his life,
With devotion and boldness, we must try to approach the Mongo
And ask them to accept new challenges for the betterment of their lives
720   We should also plead with *Ngiambe* not to take revenge on the Mongo
For that is our role, our duty to the living
But whatever the Creator chooses to do He would still be
Within His legitimate right."
After a lengthy debate, a delegation was formed
725   To look for ways to reconcile the Mongo with *Ngiambe*
One day in the season of maize and peanut harvest,
Black clouds descended on people who were attending a harvest festival

Screams rent through the black garment of the cosmos and were heard from far,
On the other side of the black lake called Maindombe,
730 Human voices bellowed into the darkness
The unknown voices proclaimed:
"*Ngiambe* has sent bandits to kill all you Mongo people,
You, your wives and your innocent children
He wants you crushed by these hooligans."
735 As the evil spirit finished saying these words,
The clouds descended very low, they became heavy
And quickly dispersed on the horizon
The forest became dark, so dark that it miraculously dried up
Birds kept silent, lions could not hunt,
740 Everything on earth became invisible
Only a very weak moon could be seen very far in the sky
Bokele, the son of Waku-Waku, knew the wrath of *Ngiambe*
He knew that his Ancestors and parents had sinned
One day, when he was entertaining some visitors,
745 They told him: "In our country, the sun has never died,
It is a big star which is bright and illuminated by the moon
Ngiambe has blessed us by beautifying the sky at night with stars."
Bokele was dazed by his own ignorance of these stars
Until then, he had never visited another country
750 Neither had he ever imagined other countries existed
He was horrified to see the land of his Ancestors turned into darkness
As Bokele was battling with thoughts of how to get back the sun,
The hostile evil spirits were celebrating their defeat of *Ngiambe*
They were hissing like snakes to show their pride
755 Bokele, ready to venture into earth itself
Decided to travel to the far ends of the earth
To buy the sun
The Mongo people, who had long claimed superiority over other groups
Now bowed down to calamity like their enemies the Sau-Sau
760 Never again would they challenge *Ngiambe*'s wisdom

Bokele Goes to Buy the Sun

Bokele made himself a canoe and said:
"I shall personally choose the creatures which will accompany me."
He chose the bees, the sparrow-hawk and the tortoise
Quietly and smoothly the canoe glided on the water and they departed,
765 They passed through green fields and forests

19

And after 200 years, they reached a country
Where they thought the sun could be sold to them
The convoy was taken to the Patriarch's palace
In line with the tradition of that country,
770   The strangers met first with the protocol lady
Who welcomed them thus:
"Come, strangers, your journey might have been long,
Come in and quench your thirst, eat and rest."
After the strangers had drunk, eaten and been entertained,
775   They were accommodated in the guest house
The following day, after they had drunk palm-wine, eaten and rested,
They were taken to the Patriarch, a man of eloquence and wisdom
As they entered the Patriarch's palace and met with him, Bokele bowed down
And saluted, saying: "Oh Patriarch,
780   Father of the great heroic tribe of the Bondonge,
I salute and pay tribute to you
Here I am, Patriarch,
With a message from your friends of all the ages, the humble Mongo people
I came with the expression of their renewed friendship and sacred word
785   To you who are known all over the cosmos and who are the most powerful
You are seated on the throne of equity, you rule with compassion,
Justice and love
You are seated where our Ancestors sat with honour and glory
You will reign in eternity like *Ngiambe* and our Ancestors
790   Patriarch, your brothers and sisters of Mongoland have a big problem,
Our problem, your Majesty, is that the sun is not seen in Mongoland
It has not been seen for the last 400 years
Majesty, your brothers and sisters suffer, you are the only one,
The only saviour who can solve their problem
795   We all know on earth and heaven that you are capable of uncountable wonders
Help, help O Patriarch! our lives are in your hands."
As he finished addressing the Patriarch in these terms,
He was invited to take a seat
The Patriarch called one of his counsellors and ordered:
800   "Take our strangers and give them a portion of our land
Give shelter and food to any Mongo who desires to live on our land
Let them in future tell the story of their migration,
Attest to future generations the bounty that is in Bondonge's land."
After the Patriarch had spoken to his counsellors,
805   All the singers, bards, drummers and poets of the country gathered
The forests, bushes and valleys resounded with welcome hymns

The fires of brotherhood sparkled throughout the country,
Greeting warmly the new friends
The Patriarch ordered his soldiers and counsellors
810 To take Bokele around the whole country
He could sense that Bokele was born of a great ancestry
For him he killed his favourite bull
Making him a feast and calling out the names of Bokele's Ancestors:
Mumaketa, Motuke, Koyambga, Lokenyo, Efoko,
815 Bowato, Bolenge and Bongwalanga
Other Mongo who were left in the darkness heard the news
They and their children now set out to join Bokele,
Wandering like beasts hit by the loss of their master
They finally reached familiar forests and rivers
820 Similar to the Mongo landscape abandoned in darkness
They cried uncontrollably for they knew that exile is always painful
They knew they would become the joke among other tribes
But they consoled themselves:
"How much better is life among strangers with light
825 Than home without the sun and the moon."
In every village they passed
The strangers were told to sleep and rest:
"Not a day in the history of our village
Have we ever closed our doors to strangers
830 Come, bring your children so that you all can rest your tired bodies
Tomorrow, we shall escort you to the neighbouring village
And from there, you will be taken to the next
Until you reach where you are going
No village shall let you continue alone"
835 After many years, they finally reached Bokele's new country
Where they all lived in happiness

Bokele Marries a Beautiful Girl

The beautiful girl from the Patriarch's family was called Bolumbu
They had many children, as many as the stars in the sky
During all these years, the Sau-Sau were busy looking for the Mongo
840 Where they had hidden themselves, nobody knew or could guess
When they finally found the Mongo,
They sent a messenger to the Patriarch
Early at dawn the evil messenger began his journey
He ran with the swiftness of a pursued antelope

21

845   And arrived at the Patriarch's country after a 50-year journey
There he reported how Bokele and his people
Had planned to kill the Patriarch
And take all his people as slaves
The Patriarch was startled at the foreboding words
850   He called his son Yakalaki to whom he told what the stranger said
Both the Patriarch and Yakalaki decided to call a meeting of the councillors
After all the councillors, the ten sages of the country, the army generals,
The soothsayers, the medicine men and women had assembled,
The stranger was asked to tell the assembly
855   What he had told the Patriarch
The stranger stood up, short and bold, to address the gathering:
"I thank you all for your warm welcome,
I thank you on behalf of the Sau-Sau people
Patriarch, you and your people are the Sau-Sau's great friends,
860   Your land is among the oldest lands history has ever known
We the Sau-Sau, and other tribes, have always respected you
We, the living and dead, will never let your country crumble
Therefore, it is wise for you to prepare for war before its slogans are heard
Do not wait until Bokele and the Mongo reduce you to ash,
865   It would be foolish to wait
Bokele has decided to attack your nation in the name of Mongo honour
He wants to elevate the Mongo reputation and make them famous
This way, he shall become the Patriarch and rule over the country."
As the stranger concluded, the eyes of those in the congregation
870   Flashed with surprise
But also fear
News spread throughout the land
That Bokele wanted to kill his father-in-law the Patriarch!
Many Kings sent their delegates to the Patriarch
875   To get the truth about the matter
The whole country threatened to disintegrate into small nations
Clamour grew, demanding Bokele's death
Bolumbu, Bokele's wife, was told to prepare poison to kill her husband
But instead she informed her husband about the plan to kill him
880   And they both decided to return to Mongoland with their children
But they needed the sun to illuminate them in Waku-Waku's land
"Let us go back, our lives are in danger," said Bokele to the animals
Which had accompanied him to the Patriarch's country
The tortoise knew that going back without sun
885   Would make life very difficult

As the whole country was deep asleep,
The tortoise went into a deep and huge grotto where the sun was kept
The bright light everywhere in the grotto blinded her
"Sun, sun, do you see me,?" she asked
890   There was no answer and there was nobody, only brighter light
That could not burn a tortoise
She continued her journey slowly but surely and got hold of the sun
Outside the grotto, drums to announce war were beaten,
From various regions of the country, regiments assembled at the hills
895   The sang battle hymns, testing their skills on open ground
They were confident, for they alone possessed the new techniques of warfa
They did not wobble like the praying mantis
They moved subtly and vigorously like crocodiles in water
Their chief commander, Madeye
900   A young man of about 35 years of age,
Announced the arrival of the Patriarch to encourage the troops
Yakalaki was among the Patriarch's entourage
They visited almost all the regiments at the hill bases
But all these preparations were in vain
905   For Bokele, his wife and children had left the Patriarch's country
The sparrow-hawk had flown with one portion of the sun
Passed to him by the tortoise,
And the bees ceremonially escorted the sparrow-hawk
New life started in Mongoland,
910   The sun started to shine again in Mongoland,
There was no darkness again in Mongoland
All the Mongo who had gone away came back to their beloved land
The first son born of Bokele and Bolumbu in the new land
Was named Lokundo Yendembe, the son who does what he wants
915   Yendembe grew in body and mind until he reached the age
To be presented to his maternal grandfather and grandmother
The day came when Yendembe had to go with his mother
To be presented to the Patriarch and his people
"Do not go alone," said Bokele to his wife
920   "Take warriors with you who will help and protect you
Yendembe should be guarded throughout the journey
Take also, this small packet in which there is magic powder
If he dies, put some powder into his nose and he will regain life."
They set off during a day of warmth and rejoicing
925   A great dawn spread its lights over the Mongo hills,
A glittering dew hung in the far blades of the valleys

Even the small plants of the dark thick equatorial forest
Broke through into light
The new season with its perfume seized Mongoland
30 The caravan peacefully and quietly continued its journey
It soared to the hill and echoed into a savannah
Yendembe and his mother decided to take a rest
They sat on a place overhung with shady trees
The whole area was filled with the song of birds
35 Bolumbu felt her mind enriched with new life,
The birds' beautiful song induced beautiful thoughts about her life
As she dozed, she dreamt a terrible dream
She saw big processions of warriors proceeding
Towards her father's home, chanting and marching
40 The Patriarch's country was deserted and himself captured
The bodies of children were strewn on the ground
Their heads smashed by gigantic creatures
Animals were eating the dead bodies
The roar echoed in emptiness
45 The whole palace was seized by a feeling of death
Amidst this horrible scene of bloodshed she heard a voice calling her:
"Bolumbu, Bolumbu, I am your grandfather Motuke
All our daughters and great sons have been slaughtered,
We have chosen you and your child to save your father's country
50 Your immediate action shall regenerate the paths of your father's country
Through your action, we shall be proud to trace our ancient paths
Get up and go now
Follow the routes leading to the Lokenyo and Efoko clans,
Take their warriors and go and defend your father's territory."
55 It was this command that woke her from the dream
After which she became troubled
There and then she ordered the caravan to depart
They followed the routes
That her grand father had told her in the dream
50 They crossed valleys and traversed plains,
Reached a place of magic where a voice asked them to stop
"Yendembe and Bolumbu, stop here and take a rest
Listen, a decision from heaven has been made by your Ancestors
Their will is that you must take back the land of your Ancestors
5   Have no fear of defeat, disaster or sadness,
You must help in building your father's nation
According to the law of infinity

You will never retreat in fear of your father's enemies
The enemies should retreat in fear of you
970   Your father's land cannot be taken by strangers
We all implore you, banish all hesitation,
Strangers must not look down upon the acts of your Ancestors
In any land, the law of the nation reigns supreme
It should never be violated, but strangers have done so
975   Whoever observes the law of the land enjoys the best of life
Though our traditions demand kindness to strangers,
This time, do not spare strangers, do not forget their secret aims,
Thus begin to prepare for tough war
Thousands of men and women will soon join in the journey."
980   As the voice stopped, an ocean appeared before the caravan
Throwing off trembling waves
When the ocean became calm,
Bolumbu and Yendembe were transfigured,
Their complexion became very light and their hair long
985   They were transported to an invisible place
Where they could see how the Patriarch's country was infested
With evil-looking beings
There were all strangers, very black in colour,
Their bodies very solid and strong and they had no hair
990   Then a Spirit came and bowed in front of Bolumbu and Yendembe
"You are a great lady and this is the son of the Patriarch's clan,
You belong to a noble and supreme clan
The strangers who have attacked your people are in search of lands
Whose earth they will scour in search of food
995   Should they then grab the land of your Ancestors?
We want you, Bolumbu and Yendembe to lead regiments of soldiers
We are sending you in order to get back that land."
After the Spirit had spoken thus, Yendembe and Bolumbu
Bowed their heads
1000 They disappeared, only to appear again far far away
Where the caravan was along the shore of the miraculous ocean
From all sides of Mongoland,
Came thousands and thousands of troops to help
Yendembe, though born only yesterday, stood on a hill and shouted:
1005 "Great Mongo warriors and friends, where you are standing now,
Beware the terror of evil strangers
Who have invaded the Patriarch's country
Who have butchered even children and women

I bear them a very deep grudge. Let us fight them
1010 I am very bitter because they have destroyed
The Holy land of the Patriarch."
As Yendembe addressed the different troops,
His father, who had been informed by the Spirits
Arrived with his own regiment, running at full speed
1015 Yendembe, in obedience and respect, bowed his head
And said to his father: "Father, you have come to join us
So that we fight and get back your father-in-law's land
Peace in the Patriarch's land will be consolidated
Peace will come through our courage and sacrifice
1020 As I talk now the country has already been destroyed
The greedy strangers are occupying all its territory
Our families in the country and even the neighbourhood
Have been annihilated and humiliated
Strangers fight their wars without war ethics:
1025 They have killed men, women, children and pets
Those who have not been killed are turned into slaves
From the voice which spoke to us here coming from this ocean,
I understand these strangers go on invading countries
Every time they are welcomed by the nation or when given hospitality
1030 Such invasions do reveal not only the enemy's greed for land
But his readiness to seize and finish whole lands."
As the young boy spoke, he was sad but solemn
His father did not say a word but made a sign of encouragement
And chanted the Patriarch's epic poem
1035 Which was soon taken up by all the troops
After they had finished reciting the Patriarch's epic poem,
The big ocean before them dried up
Evening came, large processions of regiments set out
Shouting war slogans in different languages
1040 Alternating with each clan and tribe they sang their songs of battle
Yendembe, his father and mother, led the troops
Following the routes the Spirits had shown them
Sometimes, they would stand on a hill watching the troops
As they marched in multitudes towards the battle ground
1045 They encouraged each other and every commander-in-chief of the ally troops:
"Great warriors, like angry lions crush your enemies," shouted Yendembe
The army went through rough terrain and descended the hills
Following the routes shown to them by Bolumbu
As they marched on into hills and mountains,

1050   The dust behind them made them disappear into the horizon:
        Anthems of different tribes echoed into the distant forests
        Bokele started to sing the Mongo anthem which was soon taken up by the troops
        The battle hymns were flung into the valley and high cliffs
        Bokele instructed the troops to rest in Bondonga's territory
1055   Where they were welcomed and protected
        Not very far from there, were encamped the enemy troops
        Bokele sent ahead Yendembe and a team of five war experts
        Requesting them to thoroughly study the positions and plans of the enemy
        Yendembe could see their every strategy
1060   Through the magic ring given to him by the Mongo Spirit
        Who had spoken to him and his mother at the side of the red ocean
        After the study, Yendembe and the team of experts made a report
        On the enemy army, its position and its weapons
        It was evening when the war experts and Yendembe returned
1065   To where they had left their troops resting
        After the five war experts finished reporting on what they had seen
        Yendembe stood up and said in a booming voice
        "I swear by the tomb of my grand father, no enemy shall survive
        Our number and physique alone shall deter the enemy
1070   You, general Sengambio and your troops you will occupy
        The lowest side of the River Lokoro
        You shall join the regiments of Ilualoma
        There, if the enemy dares to cross the Lokoro river,
        You shall chop him up like the teeth of a crocodile
1075   General Eyo Elinga and his troops will go to the upper side of the river
        General Bailenge and his men will hide in the forest
        Along the boundaries between the Patriarch's country
        And that of the Sau-Sau
        General Etunga will take his soldiers to the Bitabe regions,
1080   Some will go Northward and others Southward
        General Isomongoli and his warriors will protect the boundaries
        Of the Patriarch's territory with the Botwa in order to bar
        The routes to the latter, who may desire to help the enemy
        My father, my mother and myself shall be at the centre of the battlefield
1085   Go now and rest and sleep a long peaceful sleep
        Tomorrow, at the first cockcrow
        You shall leave this territory here
        And join the territory assigned to you
        You shall stand on your strong feet
1090   Till you are given the command to attack

Your duty is to break without mercy the skull of the enemy."
All night long, Bokele and Bolumbu did not sleep
They invoked their Ancestors and Spirits in song and incantation
The Ancestors and Spirits blessed the troops
1095 At first cockcrow, Yendembe called out to the troops:
"Great and powerful warriors, let us go
And prepare for the great battle
Soon we will boast of the great war tactics we shall see
Tomorrow a party shall be thrown for you."
1100 When all the warriors had come together,
Bokele spoke thus to the assembled troops:
"We shall attack together at one go like bees
We shall repulse the enemy troops
Beating them back without mercy."
1105 By the second crow of the cock
Bokele was closely followed by Yendembe, Bolumbu and the generals
Softly singing the war songs of Mongo
When they arrived at the lower ford of the river, Bokele instructed them all to stop
There they studied how to pluck the enemy army like ripe bananas
1110 Each general led the warriors under his command
Bolumbu pointed her fighting spear in the direction of the enemy army
And said: "None of the enemy soldiers will escape this spear."
Each division then set out to their assigned posts
How beautiful it was to see muscled bodies in great numbers
1115 Departing in groups towards different directions
Bolumbu roamed all over the place, ready to start the war
Had she heard the command from her husband, she would have commenced
And decimanted half of the enemy army
The day was born and soon stretched its horizons
1120 The skies opened wide adorned with multicoloured tails of dawn
The sun appeared to illuminate the minds of the earth
It lashed on the rivers, forests, mountains and hills
The morning dew evaporated suddenly from leaves and grass
Leaving behind soft and perfumed scent of wild Mongo grass
1125 Which would soon be drenched with human blood
Everything at a far distance was now visible, lit by the brightness of day
The great fig trees near the battlefield stretched deeply
Their roots into the earth
The shields, spears and arrows of the enemy army opened
1130 They flowed from North, South, East and West like rain
Most of the enemy soldiers were warriors of fame

Who knew sophisticated war techniques and plans
They carried with them bundles of high calibre weapons
They attacked while singing victory songs and anthems
1135 Yendembe, his mother and father were hidden
At the heart of the battlefield
Bokele blew a war trumpet to alert his troops
A second time he blew the trumpet
And at the third call all his warriors rushed at the enemy troops
1140 Who also were ready for the fierce fight
Bolumbu, Yendembe's mother, now opened the battle centre
She spun her spear in her hand, chasing an enemy commandant
Bokele covered his wife's back as thousands of enemies closed in on her
Waves of soldiers burst on them like angered lions
1145 But Bokele's troops drove them back
Making them retreat onto a far mountain ridge
Where they crowded together in confusion
Bokele's troops followed them on to the mountain ridge,
They chased the hordes of fleeing troops through the mountains
1150 And the whole army of warriors of fame broke up
Scattered in the mountains and hills
Seeking shelter in anthills and burning bushes
Near the boundaries with the Botwa
General Isomongoli led his warriors from the remote side of the mountains
1155 Bordering the Mongo and the Botwa,
And through the rear route they finished all the enemies
In disarray, some fled to neighbouring territory,
Others dumped their shields and other ammunition in the nearby river
They ran headlong into the thick equatorial forest
1160 Where general Bailenge's men easily captured them
Thus were avenged the Patriarch and his country
Bokele's army, singing triumphant songs,
Marched throughout the battlefield
Under the shadows of trees, they rested in the Patriarch's town
1165 Yendembe gave the dead the powder of life
And all the dead men, women and children, including the Patriarch, regained life
The Patriarch then addressed the regiments
Who had fought for his country
And the people sang in one happy voice of victory
1170 It was Bolumbu who led the gathering in different songs
From all the tribes, the crowds sang again and again:
"We have conquered the bandits

With the help of the very good warriors from the sister countries
Who can attack again the Patriarch's country?
1175 Let all the warriors remain in this land, marry and have children,
Let our country welcome all who have fought for its survival."
The crowds sang and slowly clapped their hands
When they saw the Patriarch brought to life again
Bolumbu, by a sign of her hands halted the song
1180 The warriors then recited poems in praise of the Patriarch
Composed by themselves after the war
Crouching low, they proffered their greetings and respect
When they had finished, the Patriarch sat down
On his left side, stood Yendembe and his mother
1185 And other dignitaries who had come for the occasion
On the Patriarch's right, stood Bokele and the Kings and generals
Whose armies had helped in the fighting
The emissaries from the Ancestors' cosmos sat in the row behind the Patriarch
The Patriarch, who usually did not speak much
1190 Stood up and bade the gathering to be seated
"I thank *Ngiambe* and our Forefathers who always care for us,"
"I thank the noble Kings and great generals from the many sister countries
I thank the many regiments who joined hands together to kill the bandits
I thank my son-in-law, his wife and son
1195 Who have brought to this country many harvests
Noble Kings, valiant soldiers, brothers and sisters
May our friendship bring to all of us peace
May it pave ways and nourish the power of our future generations
In all our lands, our children will multiply
1200 They will hold in reverence the sanctity of their Ancestors' name
Let this day be remembered by all mortals, Ancestors and Spirits
This land you have fought for and reconquered is ours
I shall slaughter for the occasion my choicest animals,
As an emblem of the brotherhood in our hearts
1205 Feel free to settle here, have land, cultivate it and harvest
For those who decide to go back to their respective countries
May you, when you reach the lands of your great people
Carry my words and expression of gratitude and blessing."
The Patriarch spoke these words softly
1210 And with great warmth
Not only was he feeling great emotion
But through these few noble words and expressions of gratitude
He hoped to convey his sincere thanks to those who had helped

Even today, people recognise that it was through *Ngiambe*
1215 And the Ancestral guidance that the Patriarch's country was born again
Poets, dancers, musicians and singers came together
And celebrated the friendship between nations
Hills, mountains, rivers, forests and bushes
Toasted each other with hymns of praise
1220 From the sunny days and nights illuminated by the moon and the stars
Came the anthems of friendship and peace
Then the multitude of people settled in the Patriarch's country
Bokele, his wife Bolumbu and their son Yendembe
Went to settle in a new land where Bokele lived for many years and died
1225 Before Yendembe decided to leave for far-off lands
In search of his own fortune
One night, Yendembe saw his father in a dream
"When you wake up in the morning," the old man told him,
"Go to the forest which is near the village,
1230 Follow the path which leads to the River Mayi
Before you reach the river, go into the forest
On the right side of the path
Set a simple trap then go back to the village."
Lokundo Yendembe wept bitterly that night but nobody could hear him
1235 Thinking his father had come back to life,
He opened the doors of his house to let him in
But only the wind howled and whistled,
Among the high branches of the palm-trees and baobabs,
Scattering dry grass on the roofs of the village houses
1240 Far from the rugged mountains, he heard a crowd of people roaring
It was as if a new village had been built there
Lokundo went back into his house and invoked his Ancestors
Then he took his knife,
And went to do what his father had told him in the dream
1245 After two days, Lokundo went to view the trap
It was during the dry season when mountains and hills spread their perfume,
Birds sing freely in the trees and animals frisk about the forest
Young boys and girls find great pleasure
Working with their mothers in the fields
1250 Then they go fishing, swimming and paddling their canoes
Dawn was just breaking
As Yendembe arrived at the spot where the trap was,
The clouds had melted and the moon gone for other duties
And there before his trap

1255 Stood a very beautiful young lady,
     Elegantly dressed, light in complexion,
     With a smooth and warm chest
     Her skin was soft as if it had never been touched by the sun's rays
     The smell of roses invaded Yendembe's nostrils
1260 His ears thundered and echoed in his mind and soul
     As he looked at the beautiful young girl, all his feelings were reflected on her face
     The brighter beams became dim and blue
     As the light changed, the young queen of beauty started to sing:
     "I am the first born of a large Spirit's family
1265 I was once made a human being and came to this cosmos
     I come to this cosmos now to confer on mankind the charm of procreation
     Through you, the Mongo people should multiply and reap abundant harvests
     The Ancestors and the Spirits are proud of you
     You, your father and mother commanded wisely the regiments
1270 Which miraculously crushed the many experienced warriors
     Sent by the evil spirits to attack the Patriarch's country
     The overflowing joys of the Ancestors
     And the Spirits have made me incarnate
     Because of your concern for mankind,
1275 You shall win another charm of life
     You and I shall perpetuate the bonds that bind the Mongo
     With their Ancestors and the Spirits."
     The mysterious girl sang, sang and sang
     The whole day and night and her voice echoed on heaven and earth
1280 Lokundo, overwhelmed with emotion,
     Let his mind turn to thoughts of love
     And responded with these words:
     "I hear you daughter of the Mongo Ancestor who is incarnate
     I hear your angelic voice, I hear your heart
1285 Like mine, it beats fast with emotion
     I am coming nearer you
     For both of us to pick up and circumscribe
     The orb of our love and visions
     We shall be determined not only to catch the bee
1290 But pluck the flowers and their petals of inner peace
     Our love and vision shall break the horizons of the earth and heaven."
     Lokundo moved nearer the beautiful mysterious woman
     And saw her shining with deep love for humanity
     And the invisible world
1295 Visible and hidden powers bonding both mankind with the Ancestors
     And generating new life

Not only in his heart, but in the souls and minds of humankind
Transformed, moulded and infused with the seeds of love and peace
Lokundo and Ilankaka, for that was her name, became man and wife
1300 But the child conceived of their happy union
Disappeared in the mother's womb after if had stayed there
For over 500 years
Itonde, the child of Lokundo and the woman Spirit Ilankaka
Could not be born the same way Mongo children are born
1305 Because of his double nature of spirit and human
Itonde had to live 500 years in his mother's womb
He had to disappear
And live in the Mongo forests
And rivers for initiation
1310 There he fed himself only on meat and fish
And for 200 years
The child Itonde led a lonely life

Itonde is Found by His Own People

Rumours about the existence of a strange man
Living in the Mongo forests and rivers
1315 Spread throughout the land of Waku-Waku and Bokele
In truth, the griots even today tell us
It was an elderly widow who first met Itonde at the pool,
When she was out fetching drinking water in her calabashes
Then at night, in a dream, she saw him again
1320 Addressing solemn assemblies of people from different cosmos
Some of these people were Mongo but others were white in complexion
They could neither speak Mongo nor could they understand it
One of the groups was busy killing children
While the man she had seen at the pool resurrected them with a white handkerchief
1325 The groups that were seated on soft armchairs were eating lion meat
Those seated on the ground were drinking palm wine from one calabash
Those standing looked tired, unhappy and unfed for many days
In the morning, the wise widow formally told Lokundo and his wife Ilankaka,
Of the dream and the strange meeting by the pool
1330 Lokundo gave some time to the diviners to interpret the dream
And then one of them stood up and said:
"This dream, my lord, is a good omen
For the entire Mongo people
Our rivers, lakes, forests and fields will feed many people,

1335 Even our enemies."
Another female diviner stood up and said:
"Sir, I concur with what my sister has revealed to you,
Our people shall remain prosperous, great and powerful
Our children shall rule over all other children
1340 And our enemies, the Sau-Sau, shall become our brothers and sisters
That man in the dream who resurrected the slaughtered children
Could be nobody but a Mongo who will do wonders for humankind."
Days, weeks, months passed and life in Mongoland went on normally
In the forests and rivers, Itonde continued to be initiated by Spirits
1345 One day, as he was sitting on the ground under a big tree
Enjoying the freshness of the trees and the beauty of nature,
A small bird began to sing near him:
"Itonde, hear this beautiful song
You will sing it to your father and mother,
1350 Soon you will live with them
This song, you will sing it to your wife
You will sing it to her when you see her for the first time
You will sing it to her when she is cooking,"
After the small bird had finished singing, Itonde also sang:
1355 "Little bird sent by my Ancestors,
I stand here to follow what you will tell me
I shall be the servant of my Ancestors and the Spirits
I shall sing, I shall join you in your mellow song."
The bird flew and came to sit on Itonde's right shoulder
1360 Again: "Itonde son of Lokundo and Ilankaka
Your initiation is over, yes it is over
I shall give you a talisman,
The talisman I shall give you
Is a small bell
1365 That talisman is the world
It contains everything,
Happiness, power, victory and wealth."
Itonde received the magic bell and examined it
In it, he saw the whole world as it was changing every day
1370 His loneliness was over, new life was beginning
He shook the bell and sang:
"Small bell, show me the way to my home
Show me the way to my new life
Show me the way that leads to my father's and mother's home
1375 Small bell, mark this day with a white stone."
A miraculous path appeared leading to Lokundo's and Ilankaka's village

Itonde followed it until he reached the place of the Patriarch's gong
It was a sacred gong that could neither be touched
Nor struck by anybody in this cosmos
380 Itonde entered the house in which the sacred gong was kept,
Took a stick and struck it forcefully
The sacred gong gave a deep ringing sound
Which was heard in *Ngiambe's* and the Ancestor's cosmos as well as in ours
Through this sound from the sacred gong,
385 Ancestors, representatives of *Ngiambe*, spirits and living Mongo
Flocked from all corners
To enter the compound of the sacred gong
The first to arrive was the third son of Lokundo's only sister
A champion in racing
390 Throughout generations, nations and kingdoms
He was loved by women, who had nicknamed him "the star of dawn."
Old ladies sought protection and moral support from him
His reputation for kindness was known throughout Mongoland
After him arrived the young girls and boys of the country,
395 Anxious to know why they were being summoned to gather
Women arrived in groups, prepared and ready for the meeting
The men arrived a little after the women had sat down on the grass,
They were followed by the cripples transported by their own children
The cowards and old persons arrived secretly one by one
400 Then came Lokundo and his wife Ilankaka
Followed by the agents of heaven and Ancestors' representatives
Itonde was there, his eyes fixed on his father and mother
Who had never seen him in his human form
Lokundo's sister's third son approached Itonde and challenged him:
405 "Who are you? Whose son are you? What is your clan?
You shall be stricken with an everlasting curse
Your body shall be cut into small pieces."
Itonde, who was sitting near the gong, stood up and murmured
Some few words to his magic bell which told him what to say:
410 "Brothers, sisters and friends, I am a real son of this land
This is my father and this is my mother."
Angered by these words, Lokundo shouted:
"I have never had a son for my wife is a spirit
Men and women, do you hear this insult from this arrogant boy?"
415 "Please father, let me talk, I am your own son and I shall prove it,"
Replied Itonde with all the respect due to a father from his son
Ilankaka replied with violence: "I have never had a child

I expected one who disappeared before it was born."
"Yes mother, I am your child
1420 Who lived in loneliness in the forest and rivers,"
Said Itonde, bowing down before his mother
"Never in my life have I ever had to lie to somebody
I have always feared the ears of my Ancestors to hear lies
I am your child,
1425 Even mountains, hills and trees are bent to hear this truth
I speak now in agreement with the Spirits and the Ancestors."
The woman who had seen Itonde at the pool and in the dream recognised him
"Twice I have seen this man, at the pool and in the dream
I can swear before assemblies of dead and the living,
1430 This is the Mongo Spirit incarnate the diviners and oracle spoke about."
All the women present accepted as truth what the speaker had said
But the men, skeptical and stubborn went on arguing
They set up a committee of elders to deliberate
What they called an offence to the Patriarch Lokundo
1435 His wife and the entire community
"Such an offence," they said, "may bring bad omen and curse
To present and future generations of Mongo
And friends here present."
After they had talked in private, it was decided
1440 That two types of poison be prepared and given to Itonde
If he died, his body would be thrown away and eaten by the dogs of the village
To prevent his evil spirit from appearing again
It was the eldest counsellor, Bamania, who announced the decision
All the girls and women cried and pleaded with the men
1445 To soften their hearts and leave the stranger in peace
But despite their sobs, cries and pleas,
Two types of poison were given to Itonde
Before taking the concoctions he shook his magic bell which sang:
"Itonde, drink this poison
1450 the Ancestors and the Spirits are with you
Drink it to show your relatives the will and plans of *Ngiambe*,
The Ancestors and Spirits
Must be fulfilled however malicious mankind may be."
After the bell had stopped singing, Itonde took over:
1455 "Indeed ultimate truths are often first refuted
Before they are accepted by mankind,
The solution is not violence, but patience
I shall drink the poison, for the Ancestors are protecting me
I shall never succumb to the evil forces of destruction

160 The promises of *Ngiambe* the Creator and the Ancestors
Must be made true in the name of all humanity
I shall drink the poison offered by my own relatives
Ancestors, I entrust myself to you
Knowing that I can pay you back very little
165 Father Lokundo, I am your real son."
The stranger bowed his head
And after paying tribute to the dead and the living
He took the cup full of poison, drank it and said:
"It is only in pursuance of the Ancestors' will
170 That I consent to drink this poison prepared by my own father."
After he had drunk the first cup of poison,
He gave thanks to *Ngiambe* and the Ancestors
He took the second cup and bowed again his head
He drank the bitter poison and tossed away the cup
175 The young women in the crowd devoured him with their eyes
They stood there watching and sympathising with him
From where he stood, he dispersed his bounty to all,
Even to those who had given him poison
Then took a big gulp of the water of life provided by the magic bell
180 After he had rested, he addressed his father and mother:
"The Spirits and the Ancestors know how to guide us,
I shall always humble myself before them."
Lokundo and his wife were breathing heavily as if they had run a race
Silence reigned through the crowds
185 Finally Lokundo stood up and said:
"Let the people know that this is the real son of Ilankaka
Who disappeared from her womb so that the Ancestors' prophesy
May come to pass."
After he had spoken thus:
190 A throne was made and Itonde was immediately crowned
Lokundo went to the throne, and with his two hands he blessed Itonde
By spitting on his head three times and saying
"Brothers , sisters and friends, Itonde is my only beloved son
Nobody in this land shall rebuke or forsake him
195 Every man, woman and child shall sing his praise
His family name shall be Ilelangonda, in short Ilele
Brothers and sisters, know that ignorance is a terrible sin
Each generation has its words of wisdom
Son Ilele, remember always that only those who feed themselves
500 Can be fed by the Ancestors

For they only provide the courage and wisdom
With which we are enabled to cross the tricky meanderings of life
The springs and deadlocks of our ideas and actions
Where the brightness of our minds and souls begins or ends
1505 I, your father, have never ignored the words and truths of our Forefathers,
You too should never ignore them all your life,
Instead, you live to reap in their fields
The seeds of past, present and future generations are full of enthusiasm
Never be blinded by our own enthusiasms
1510 You, the intermediary between the living and the Forefathers,
You ought to be the wisest of the nation
You, being wiser than all under your rule and authority,
Must pace not before, but behind, watching everybody's footsteps
You should also know, son, however clever you are,
1515 However fast you run the race of life,
Do not deceive yourself to earn the love of all your people
However much you may give,
However generous you may be,
None of these actions will satisfy people's appetites
1520 They will pass through the back door into your bedroom
Breaking tradition and allowing themselves the liberty
Of roaming at will
Until finally they shall forge ways and means
Of knowing the inner secrets of your bowels!
1525 These words, son, I received from my father,
I pass them on to you knowing that you will also pass the torch
To illuminate generations and generations of mankind."
After Lokundo had uttered these words of truth and wisdom,
A tumultuous roar of shouts and praise was heard
1530 From the ecstatic congregation
Women shouted words of encouragement to Itonde
A young girl of 13 leapt high up into the air
She was followed by the greatest poetess, Mbilia
Who celebrated the occasion with poems she had composed herself
1535 Chanting slowly, not wasting her words, she danced leisurely
Turning herself in circles and moving her body gracefully,
Eager to exhibit her poetic talents and skills
Her tuft of hair and her naked breasts moved gently like waves in the sea
The feast went on for many days, weeks and months
1540 Ilelangonda never imagined he would inherit such glory
From the very people who had given him poison to swallow

38

Although he had been fed poison, Ilele had no grudge against his people
For he knew it was the prophesy of the Ancestors
In his deepest heart, love soothed all injuries
545   He thought only of the good deeds
He had planned to do for the Mongo people
He thought of how he could make humankind
Die with a full awareness of *Ngiambe*'s will and desire
He thought of ways to make people understand
550   That no creature on earth was allowed to destroy *Ngiambe's* gifts
He knew that man very often forgot
That the destruction of *Ngiambe's* creation was a sin against life
But he was pleased to learn that among the Mongo
There were some who feared *Ngiambe* and obeyed Him
555   He said to himself: "Today we all here have our hearts
Full of happiness and joy because of my rebirth in this cosmos,
But how long will this happiness and joy last?
If the people are bound unswervingly to their faith in *Ngiambe*,
By my effort they shall overcome all the evil forces
560   I shall do my best to make human beings acquire from *Ngiambe*
The powers of discernment and perception
I shall do my utmost for them to know eternity
Whose cycles of life never cease or stop
I shall make them obey the Creator
565   Who makes all truths turn into eternity and immortality
During my leadership in this world of the living,
I will fill the land with abundance and growth
And the scent of the yellow roses will uplift the minds and thoughts
Of humble beings issued from all the races
570   No righteous one will wander in the wide expanse of this earth
And all the dwellings will be illuminated
By the innumerable heavenly bodies of wisdom
The hearts of all the righteous shall always be filled with joy
Together they shall live and together they shall fight
575   All things in the universe that are bad
Shall regain their beauty by mankind's good deeds
Beautiful things shall not fade,
But, shall remain beautiful until the end of all time."
These were the thoughts Ilele had as he started his life among the living
580   But he was not discouraged for he knew
That human beings of courage
Would survive the evil spirit's holocaust

The Spirits would renew their strength
And increase their faith and powers
1585 So that *Ngiambe's* mysterious movements of creation
Shall never end, neither shall they be stopped by Munguna[11]
Ilele knew that the love of creation has always inspired all creatures
And made them strong enough for any fight on this earth
By his faith, mankind is linked to *Ngiambe*, the Almighty
1590 Ilele was not afraid of the realities of the world
For he knew that all people become mature through experience
When old and matured by various experiences,
The Ancestors and the Spirits shall infuse them with wisdom
From which is created the language of knowledge
1595 That shall be the means of communication between the living,
Their Ancestors, the Spirits and *Ngiambe*
This language, if acquired without knowledge and wisdom,
Is no longer a symbol of communication
It causes death without mercy
1600 And it exposes the emptiness, the lack of wisdom and knowledge
Of the very people who speak it,
Regardless of their age, power, wealth or social position
In such a case, the union and interaction between the living,
The Ancestors, the Spirits and *Ngiambe* cannot exist
1605 It is in the nature of this earth that such communities should exist
Because mankind is always targeted by evil spirits
Who prevent the acquisition of the language of knowledge
Often times the living resign and surrender to the evil spirits
That seize the human intellect
1610 And dictate a course deviated from the common path of truth
This is the main reason for which our cosmos is hit by *Ngiambe*
His command is that when we are hit, we should call upon Him
Because He can restore life
As Ilele sat on the base of the throne inherited from his father
1615 And as he struggled with all these truths and thoughts,
He saw in his mind a riot of colour
He felt his head uplifted in defiance of evil forces
Seething with faith in *Ngiambe's* promises and wonders,
Always remembering that wherever he would be
1620 The Ancestors' good eyes would see him
After Ilele had rested his soul and mind,
After his boiling nerves had cooled down,
He remembered that too much thinking makes for little action

And that for him to speak the language of wisdom and knowledge
625 On behalf of the assemblage of heaven and earth,
He needed to combine both action and thought
Nobody on earth would listen to many thoughts
Without concrete and useful actions
Aware of this, he concluded he would always reconcile both
630 At the time these deep thoughts were settling in Ilele's mind,
All the eyes of the living and the dead were focused on him
For in him was contained their hope and trust
That is why *Ngiambe* did not give him normal eyes and a normal mind
Indeed, Ilelangonda's eyes were bright with courage and wisdom
1635 Before they departed to their respective homes,
Ilelangonda had this to say:
"Brothers and sisters,
Any life granted by *Ngiambe* must let loose all its powers
In His honour and glory for it to be beautiful and meaningful
1640 We who are chosen by Himself *Ngiambe* the Creator,
We who have truly inherited His grace,
We to whom He gave a complete body and intelligence,
We should always give the exact meaning of life
We should teach ourselves the totality of that meaning
1645 We must learn from the Ancestors and the Spirits
How to thank *Ngiambe* for our achievements
However simple or sophisticated this may appear
Our role as the proteges of *Ngiambe*, the Ancestors and the Spirits
Is to make the course of eternity predictable as planned by *Ngiambe*
1650 We should ensure that the union of things does not disintegrate
And that it should translate the true essence of creation
Not because we are Mongo or any other tribe,
Not because we want to equate ourselves with Ancestors,
But because we have a glimpse of the real feelings of *Ngiambe*
1655 Though we are at the centre of His creation,
Our intelligence remains so limited
That we become narrow-minded beings in His hands
Whatever happens in this cosmos of ours is part of our being
Because we are the bonds binding all creatures together
1660 If we arouse the wrath of *Ngiambe*,
And if we do not make any effort to do His will
Then our life shall be doomed to failure for millennia
All the seeds planted during many years by different generations
Shall decay and the expected fruits shall wither

1665   Therefore, those of us who do not believe in these truths,
       Thinking they are merely the talk of every day,
       Will see the bitterness of their own deceit,
       The foolishness and uselessness of their perceptions
       Great people of *Ngiambe*, these words should prod us
1670   Into good actions at all times and for ever
       Let us remind ourselves that reckless behaviour
       By one living being can make the world crumble,
       That simple neglect of our tasks is an abominable crime
       Ngiambe, the Ancestors and the Spirits know the threats of life,
1675   Let us trust that they shall always protect mankind."

SECOND NIGHT

Lokundo lived a little longer than 500 years
His face filled with wrinkles and he became very tired
He knew he would join his Ancestors very soon
One day during the season of peanut harvest
5   He called a meeting of the elders and the councillors
The griots, the medicine women, the diviners, the fishermen and the hunters
Ilelangonda and his mother Ilankaka were also invited
As the sun dimmed its ancient light
Great processions of councillors assembled
10   One by one they passed in front of Lokundo
Their heads bowed in respect
The griots, ornamented with beads of different colours
Recounted the epics of the Mongo
And festooned rose flowers
15   Round the necks of Lokundo, his wife and Ilele
They sang the fame of Waku-Waku and other Mongo heroes
The Spirits and the Ancestors chose from among the congregation
Illelangonda as their favourite who would take over from Lokundo
They thrust sun beams on Ilelangonda
20   Who was honoured by the whole congregation
His father, Lokundo, stood up to speak:
Assisted by two aides who held him from both sides
"I salute you in the name of our Ancestral Forefathers
I salute you on behalf of the living Mongo wherever they are
25   I salute you in the name of our children yet to be born
I salute you on behalf of my wife
And that of our child Ilele
I am proud of our Ancestors who have kept me all these years
I have the humility to ascertain that I have fulfilled
30   The tasks assigned to me by them
Though sometimes with imperfection
I now bring to them and to you a noble present
Ilele, my only son
Who has been chosen to be the flower, the light
35   And the leader
Whose wisdom and rule shall go beyond
The boundaries of Mongoland
Through you Ilele, many Mongo families
Will reach their destiny

40	And through you, our stories, epics and traditions shall continue
	The whole congregation here present and absent
	Has come to give you blessings
	And infuse you with eagerness, courage and sense of humour
	Whoever here present or absent believes
45	In the Mongo people's progeny
	And shall partake in the fruit harvest of his trust
	And loyalty to the Ancestors
	Through you, the Mongo shall continue multiplying
	Whenever I shall be, I will ask the Ancestors to guide you
50	But before I depart to our Forefathers' home
	I want to bless your marriage
	Look for a girl to marry
	And I shall be proud to pay the dowry."
	The news spread throughout the land
55	That Ilele was looking for a girl to marry
	Big and small nations
	Empires, kingdoms, families and clans
	All sent contingents of girls to Lokundo's palace
	So that Ilele could make his choice
60	A committee of selection was organised
	Which shortlisted beautiful girls
	From whom the jury retained one
	But Ilele rejected their choice saying he wanted to marry
	A girl he himself had met, talked with and loved
65	Lokundo was angry and frustrated
	But could not change his son's decision
	"Go anywhere you want and find yourself a wife
	As young Mongo men have always done
	The clan and the tribe will accept her as a daughter-in-law
70	Go my son, I wish you the best of luck."
	It was on the following day
	The day after his father had addressed him
	That Ilele set out to look for a girl to marry
	He proceeded North where he was sure to find one
75	As he traversed rivers, mountains and hills
	He turned over in his mind
	The wise words his father had always told him
	He knew that without a wife
	His people would not accept him as their leader
80	After all, didn't his father warn him

That the Mongo sun would not end with him!
He was alarmed at the thought of the Ancestors' wrath
If he did not fulfil their plans
On the other hand, he had to get married
85   While his father was still alive
And he appealed to the Ancestors to keep his father alive longer
Whenever he saw his agemates who were already married
His heart was torn with pain
But Ilele did not curse the earth
90   Neither did he utter a word of anger
Instead, with courage, he went on searching
He was determined to find a girl to marry
One afternoon, Ilele met a group of girls dancing
Their voices echoed in his lovelorn heart
95   He stood and watched them for a while
Though they were singing and dancing to tunes unknown to him
Ilele suddenly leapt into the arena
And joined the dancing girls
The very movements of his hips and buttocks
100   Described the problem in his mind
As he danced away like one of the girls
The village people asked what boy was this
Who danced like a girl
He bent down, turned around, beat the earth
105   And shook his shoulders with hands akimbo
This dance and all the sounds renewed his mind and soul
And rose with the high winds of hope and expectation
He felt the power to see beyond the clouds of life
He could see himself in future times
110   He could hear the solemn voices of his Forefathers
He could address things and make them acquire eternal life
As he danced and sang with the unknown girls
His spirit was no longer befuddled by confusing thoughts
His voice joined those of the girls in song
115   Thundering far out into the distance
They sang and smiled at one another
Like lovers on their honey-moon
Dispelling the black clouds of despair
That had settled in Ilele's heart
120   He then discovered among his dance-partners a beautiful girl
Whose physique was the most attractive

Her body smooth and soft
She looked at Ilele tenderly
And smiled with heart-felt emotion
125 Had he landed on the tree that would bear fruit?
Yes, she was all woman but was she created
To be the mother of a hero?
A new generation to be born in the land of Lokundo
Ilele mingled with the people of the village
130 But created for himself an opportunity to talk to the girl
"I have come for you."
"For me? Why?"
"I want to marry you. I want you to be my wife."
"Your wife? What do you mean by your wife?
135 A first wife? A second one? Or just for the occasion?"
Replied the girl
The conversation had not gone far before Ilele realised
That he could not marry this girl
For, like him, she was of two natures
140 Part spirit and part human being
Such people recognise their kind very easily
For they possess marks on their faces
Which are invisible to ordinary mortals
But visible to themselves
145 Ilele left and went to another village
As he was entering the village
He met a man covered with palm-oil
From his head to his feet
Ilele stopped him and asked him what had happened
150 The man replied that he was coming from a nearby village
Where he wanted to marry a girl called Mbombe
The most beautiful, the most intelligent
And the most hardworking girl of the region
But according to her tradition
155 Marriage with her could only be possible
If a suitor defeated her in a wrestling match
That took place in a pool of palm-oil
Wide of three meters, long of four and deep of two
The man, having been defeated twice by Mbombe, could not marry her
160 No more chances would be given to him all his life
Many other boys and men had tried
And now lived with the bitterness of defeat and rashness

46

Nobody in the cosmos of the living had ever defeated Mbombe
The most beautiful girl of the region
165   The best wrestler of all time
But Ilele took the challenge and went to talk to her:
"Are you Mbombe, the most beautiful girl in the region?
The most gentle girl this cosmos has ever had?
The most hard-working person among the Mongo people
170   I love you, I want to marry you," said Ilele
"And I, too, love you
You are a very handsome boy
You look strong, stout and powerful
I want to be your wife and live with you in great happiness
175   But the tradition of this land has it that
Before I can be your wife, you should defeat me in a wrestling match
If you agree, I shall introduce you officially to my people."
Ilele agreed to be taken to Mbombe's parents and relatives
Since the wrestling match in the pool of palm-oil
180   Had not yet taken place
No preferential treatment could be given to him
The two parties only agreed on the date and time
When the wrestling match would take place

The Miraculous Wrestling Match

The day of the match dawned bright and sunny
185   Mbombe's father turned to his wife and said
"Such a day is often accompanied
By many other unusual events
It shall be loaded with showers of blessing
And thunder-storms of celebration."
190   The old man spoke jokingly but he could feel the sense of expectation
Among the crowd and between the two wrestlers
Drums were beaten to pass on the news of the big match
All the bells rang, the birds in the trees sang
The cats of the village miaowed and the dogs barked
195   Monkeys in the forest jumped from tree to tree
Lions stopped roaring
And the gazelles frisked about gracefully
Slaves from various villages were assembled
To sweep the empty pool with palm-leaves
200   Men, women and children carried kegs of palm-oil to fill the pool

47

The slaves, after sweeping the pitch (pool), poured in palm-oil
Then the two wrestlers were brought
Mbombe looked around at everybody and smiled
Cheered and encouraged by the numerous peoples of Mongoland
205   She removed her skirt made of raffia
Her physique attracted an ocean of curious male eyes
The crowd chanted:
"You who has defeated all men
Where now shall you send this Patriarch's grandson?
210   O! where else can we find a brother and a son-in-law?
You who defeated all men, tell us."
And an elderly woman commented aloud:
"I know, this boy is going to be our son-in-law
We love him, he shall win."
215   Ilelagonda was sweating in anticipation
But he looked strong and powerful
Boldly he moved towards Mbombe, stared at her
And said: "I am going to defeat you" Lets begin
The girl of great fame followed him fearlessly into the pool
220   The assembly booed and whistled
Mbombe uttered some inaudible words and opened wide her mouth
She got hold of the stranger but could not throw him
Mbombe's muscles were trembling like sea waves
Her hair tied down like husks of millet grains
225   She prayed for a while then suddenly threw herself on Ilele
Twisted his head, squeezed his nose and lifted him
But Ilele refused to fall
"Father Lokundo," he implored
"Should I not marry this girl
230   Who I so dearly love
Should the bonds binding me with the Ancestors be broken?
I would rather be killed
Than disappoint the Mongo Spirits and Forefathers."
After he had prayed thus he took a deep breath
235   Concentrated on his powers and strength
Then he seized Mbombe by her wrists
Pinned them down and murmured:
"Ilelangonda, son of Lokundo
Be strong, do not give up
240   Remember the promise of your Forefathers."
His strength boiled in his veins

He threw all his weight on the girl
But Mbombe neither moved nor shook
Ilele squeezed her nose, blocked her breath
245 Then seized her up on his huge shoulders
And threw her on her back like a log of wood
Mbombe sank in the pool of oil
Ilele dived and brought her to the surface
The crowd shouted in praise of Ilele:
250 "The miraculous wrestling match is over
Mbombe has at last found a man
Who is going to make her happy all her life
The women of Mongoland are now liberated
Mbombe and Ilele have chosen their destiny without fear."
255 The lions roared and shook the earth in triumph
The ocean waters beat the sand of the shores in triumph
The beautiful women of Mbombe's clan came together
To organise the marriage ceremony
Mbombe's mother was exuberant with joy
260 Distributing freely her laughter
Poems of excellence were recited
Songs of marriage were chanted
The pride of the Mongo people had been restored again
The spring of life flowed now even in the wilderness
265 From the womb of Mbombe, would be born a Mongo hero
Who according to the prophesy
Would speak a different language
That of peace and unity among all the tribes in the land
The whole nation began to radiate with new life
270 And Ilele made friends throughout the region
He was not only respected, but liked as an intelligent man
Whose child would liberate the Mongo from their enemies
A man of determination and courage
A man of thoughts
275 A man who had paved the way for future Mongo generations
An obedient man who had accepted the duties assigned to him
By the Ancestral Forefathers
An intermediary between the past and new generations
These truths Ilelagonda knew
280 The spirits had told him during his initiation
In the forests and waters
And his father had told him the day he was enthroned

He knew he was a perpetuator
Of Mongo tradition and leadership
285 From the gates of all the four cosmos
The Ancestral Forefathers
Waited for their emissaries
Who had gone to watch the wrestling match
They knew that the marriage between Ilele and Mbombe
290 Had been concluded
But they wanted to hear it from the months of the messengers
From afar, they heard them singing, chanting and rejoicing
Ngiambe the Creator in His cosmos watched with keen interest
He watched the Ancestors rejoice and laugh
295 He watched the living Mongo dance, sing, eat, drink
And He heard their booming laughter
He watched the wicked tribes hit by sadness and misery
Their heads bowed to the ground
Unable to wipe away their tears
300 He watched the Spirits educating their children
By showing them the paths of wisdom
Ngiambe heard every day
These children pray to Him with faith:
"*Ngiambe* the moulder of the visible and the invisible
305 Grant peace and love and creativity to all your creatures
May they not hate, kill or despise one another
May they always do your will like our mothers and fathers."
Through these prayers and appeals
Ngiambe was made more powerful
310 He marvelled at the bounty of his creation
And sent abundant harvests
And life to the cosmos of the Mongo people
Because of these appeals and prayers
Ngiambe made the righteous among the Mongo rise
315 He called upon people like Waku-waku, Lokundo
Ilele and others
To strengthen and perpetuate the bonds of families
Tribes and countries
After watching the Mongo, the Spirits
320 And the Ancestors in their cosmos
Ngiambe concluded aloud: "By my power and will
The evil spirits
Will never conquer those among humankind

Who remain faithful to me
325 And plant the seeds of love and unity."
These were the words *Ngiambe* uttered
To bless Ilele and Mbombe's union
These were the words which eternally bond *Ngiambe* to his creatures
These were words which give life to real life
330 Ilele continued to entrust himself to *Ngiambe*
And to the Ancestors
He continued to appeal for better leadership from them
He continued to live in his-in-laws village
Meditating upon the wonders of *Ngiambe* and the Ancestors
335 Then one day he rose at dawn to talk to his father-in-law
Ilele entered the round house
Where Mbombe's father was waiting
The old man knew his son-in-law was not only for Mbombe
But for all generations
340 And therefore, he had to be listened to carefully
With an open mind
Ilele was the custodian, the keeper
The preserver of mankind's symbols
The star that would reside in the Mongo children's eyes
345 Nobody doubted that such powers
Came from *Ngiambe* the Creator
From the spirits and from the Ancestors
"Father," said Ilele, "I want to go home with my wife
I want her to meet my father, my mother and my relatives
350 I want my wife to know where the sun rises and where it sets
I want my father to bless our union
Before he goes to the Ancestors'
I want my father to pay the dowry as he promised."
Mbombe's father did not object
355 After all his daughter had to follow her husband
Eighty strong men were chosen to escort Ilele and his wife
The caravan waited for the first fruit of the sun
Mbombe, Ilele and the 80 strong men
Left the village of the wrestling match
360 Ilele knew that his father, mother and relatives
Were waiting to see the girl he had chosen for himself
A girl of plentifulness, selflessness and greatness
A girl of bravery, courage and without self praise
A girl of kindness, power and sense of humour

365	A great girl whose fame was celebrated
	Among the living and the dead
	The caravan continued its journey
	Fifteen nights whispered
	Until they were taken over by 15 days
370	By then Mbombe was tired and restless
	"Ilele my husband," she said, "Why don't we take a rest here
	Build our house and live in this lovely forest here."
	"Yes my dear wife, let us build our house here,"
	Replied Ilele with tenderness, compassion and love
375	"But before we settle in this forest
	We need to offer a sacrifice of settlement."
	After the sacrifice to the Ancestors
	A palm-tree was planted
	Ilelangonda made himself a drum to send a word to his father
380	He beat the drum: "Father, I am back home
	Mother, I am back home
	No wise man can hide meat from fire
	I am back to present you the girl I have married
	You must see my wife and pay the dowry, I am back
385	We are resting now, we shall come, we shall come home."
	The forest was cool, calm and vast
	The sky was cloudy and dark
	The clouds played acrobatic games across the sky
	Sometimes they changed into one small cloud
390	That looked like a lady
	Sometimes they became an old man with a hat on his head
	Sometimes smaller clouds melted and gave birth to bigger ones
	Which merged to look like an animal
	Mbombe sat under a tree enjoying the beauty of nature
395	The 82 travellers departed
	They walked leisurely following the many paths in the forest
	Until they reached the bended bushes of beasts and ogres
	Mbombe had kept a magic-cat skin
	Given to her by her father
400	On the eve of the miraculous wrestling match
	She spread it on the ground and invited her husband
	And the 80 strong men from her village to sit on it
	Then she said: "Father's magic cat's skin, take us away
	Fly very high in the sky and clouds
405	Let us not be attacked by the ogres

Take us home to my father-in-law's
He is looking forward to receiving us"
The magic skin on which they were seated flew very high
The beasts and ogres on the ground stood transfixed
410   Knowing they could do nothing to harm people
Transported by a magic vessel
The magic mat disappeared into the sky
It travelled in the clouds
After they had journeyed in space for three months
415   The magic skin smoothly and gently landed in Ngimokili, their destination
Lokundo's people were ready to welcome them
They gave gold, diamonds, crops and cattle
To their sister and daughter-in-law
As a way of welcoming her into the clan
420   Mbombe was accepted by the living and the dead
All glory and honour were hers in Lokundo's village
Feasts were held in Ngimokili
Celebrating the marriage between one man and one woman
Between families, clans, tribes and countries
425   Lokundo and his wife opened wide their hearts
To their son and new daughter-in-law
Ordering their relatives and servants
To accommodate the couple in the best palace
Great was the ceremony of marriage between Mbombe and Ilele
430   The crowds kicked up a din
Which reverberated through forests and hills
Young women were filled with the joy
Of preparing for such an unprecedented union
They cooked great quantities of food for the invitees
435   Some sat in groups to plait their hair
Others learned and practised new and old dances
Old women chatted about the future of their children
They thought how great too their daughters'
And sons' weddings would be
440   Celebrated and danced at Ngimokili Village
Ngiambe was represented by Elima Mosantu
Ngabriela also was there
Moyizi too was there
Abrahamu was there with Petelo
445   All *Ngiambe*'s favourites came that day
Then Satana, uninvited, appeared at the fete

There was a commotion when the feasting people saw him
So embarrassed was he that he decided to leave
People at the fete wondered what man Satana was
450   Who had no sense of shame
A man who incarnates all evil, death and misery
A dirty pig with a tail like a baboon
The time came when Ngabriela gave more powers to Ilele
And declared him Lokundo's successor
455   As he stood up to speak, people saw his radiant face
Spreading the grace he received from *Ngiambe*
Ilele and Mbombe were brought before him
They knelt down and Ngabriela laid his hands on them:
"As from today, Ilele is no longer a child, but a man
460   Mbombe is no longer a girl, but a woman
For the living, Ilele is a leopard, a symbol of power
For the Ancestors, he is the intermediary
Between them and the living
Through him, peace shall prevail in this land
465   *Ngiambe* has asked me to announce on his behalf
That through Mbombe and Ilele, nations shall be united
Through Mbombe and Ilele, even enemy tribes shall unite
Through Mbombe and Ilele, peace and unity shall prevail."
As she listened to these words
470   Mbombe saw brighter light in her spirit and mind
She realised that the mission before her was not easy
Henceforth, she had to watch, listen and behave with dignity
After Ilele, Mbombe, Lokundo and his wife had lived
For many years in Ngimokili,
475   The land became less fertile,
The rivers and the forest dry
Ilelangonda decided to call a meeting of the whole village
To inform them of his intention to settle elsewhere
The whole concourse of villagers shouted:
480   "We shall always live with you
We shall follow you wherever you will be
We shall serve you all our lives."
A new place was identified by the elders and the counsellors
New houses were built by each family and clan
485   And the Ngimokili people moved to a place called Nkuma
There, life was easy because there was plenty of food
Fish, meat, fruit, cassava, plantain, there was in abundance

Above all, the great happiness of the Mongo was Mbombe's pregnancy
Announced formally by five sages
490   During the feast of hunting and fishing
Mbombe's pregnancy was a great event for all Nkuma people
Because they knew that if Mbombe did not bear that child
The Mongo people would be misled by evil spirits
Mbombe's pregnancy was proof that *Ngiambe* had not forgotten
495   His promise to mankind
Indeed, even today, no living or dead Mongo could doubt
The truth of *Ngiambe's* promise
Because they knew that He always gave
His action to His own word
500   Through Mbombe's pregnancy, *Ngiambe* made the Mongo
Know the full meaning of their lives
In His honour and glory, Mongo high priests
Held prayers of thanksgiving:
"You who are the giver of the truth of procreation
505   Bless the homes of those who honour and glorify your name."
Divine songs were sung that echoed over the hills and valleys
Various musical instruments whispered *Ngiambe's* name
And all the people of the land
Men, women and children prayed
510   There were vows of obedience and faith to *Ngiambe*
And all the soil became more fertile
Fish swelled in the rivers, lakes and lagoons
Yes, Mbombe's pregnancy opened the hearts of all beings
New visions and new hopes brought new petals
515   Doubts, despair and hatred disappeared from Mongoland
Evil and misfortune led to poems of love and laughter
Those Mongo who had lost their faith repented
And gave their lives to *Ngiambe*
They knew that to achieve perfection they had to obey Him
520   Serve Him and live in harmony with their neighbours
Mbombe became very tired, bearing in her womb
The long awaited child, who still had not been born
More than two generations of women
Who conceived after Mbombe, had delivered
525   And their children had matured, married and died
But Mbombe still kept her pregnancy
The people of Nkuma became impatient
They laughed at Mbombe and said:

"Eh, eh, eh that one who is carrying her pregnancy on the ground
530   When is she going to deliver?
Is it really a child or a tumor?
And those women who were jealous
Spoke of her only with bitterness of heart
But Mbombe did not care what those full of hatred
535   And envy were saying
She knew that some Nkuma people were distorting
The substance of the truth
She was consoled because she knew
She was bearing a boon for humankind
540   She knew she had to fulfil the promise of *Ngiambe*
And that the wicked and foolish are always first
To utter words of destruction
Although there were those who had no opinion
There were also those who were driven
545   To castigate the unborn hero's mother
And those who could not understand
How some people in Nkuma Village
Could utter such spiteful pronouncements of blame to Mbombe
Nor could they understand why
550   Mbombe bore them no resentment
When she had all the powers and means of punishment
But Mbombe did not revenge for she believed in the greatness
And the might of heavenly judgement
The truth was simple
555   The hero could not be born like any human child
For he was a Spirit who had accepted to become flesh
All news, good or bad, reached Ilele's ears
And when he heard what was said about Mbombe
He wished the Ancestors would send again somebody
560   To help the Mongo people understand *Ngiambe's* plan
Not to lose their faith as they had before
Ilelangonda feared that should the ill-natured words
Of his people continue
The Ancestors and *Ngiambe*
565   Would cast darkness over Nkuma
He decided to call a meeting of the men and women living in Nkuma
"Sons and daughters of our Forefathers," he said
"The direction of our lives these days is distorted
Ngiambe and the Ancestors will punish us

570 If we do not change our ways
Our lives shall turn into vast pools of blood
Remember how in ancient times, darkness hit Mongoland
The moon and sun sank and brought fierce nights
This time, brothers and sisters, *Ngiambe's* wrath
575 Will surpass its limits
We must stop indulging in speculation
And instead, seek the truth
Man's creation issues from Himself *Ngiambe*
Therefore, it is not for us here on earth
580 To challenge His wisdom
Our arguments on the birth of the hero
Show our lack of trust in Him
Who on this cosmos can oppose His truth about creation?
Those who have tried
585 Have done so to their own detriment
Whatever argument we have on the hero's birth
Create a threat unto ourselves
To our children and the children of our children to be born
Let us not lay fears in our hearts
590 Let us trust in *Ngiambe*
The hero shall appear on the day *Ngiambe* has promised."
The congregation listened with open hearts and ears
Even those who spoke ill of Mbombe did not quite hate her
Though they may have said some things out of jealousy
595 Similar meetings were held
By the elders, chiefs of clans and tribes
To explain in simple words what Ilele had spoken about
They sought better understanding of the truth
And to reassure the people
600 Fresh seeds of love were planted in their hearts
Gossip died off and rumour-mongers were silenced
But something was disturbing Ilele's peace of mind
Something was paining him
Something was rotting in Ilele's heart:
605 Mbombe had refused to eat food
She had also refused to drink water
The best cooks were hired to prepare food for her
But still she refused
The smell of any food made her vomit blood
610 Sometimes Ilele would try to spoon feed her

She would swallow a mouthful of plaintain with meat
But she would vomit for the rest of the day
Her health became a big problem for the people of Nkuma
One day, after she had vomited for many hours in her bedroom
615 Ilele took her outside the house
Both sat under the shade of a baobab tree
Talking about the vomiting disease
That had saddened the whole of Nkuma
Suddenly came a strange bird
620 Flying in the sky above their heads
The bird was a big and long-billed calao
People came out of their houses to look at it
It was the first time such bird had been seen in Mongo skies
The elders of Nkuma demanded that their hunters should kill it
625 The whole village was surprised
And frightened by the presence of that strange bird
All wondered what calamity it was bringing to Nkuma!
Impatiently they observed the two-billed bird
Flying over their village
630 Then it came to a standstill above Mbombe's house
Majestically, it opened its bill, and threw down a fruit
Round like an egg
Mbombe stood up, picked it and showed it to Ilele
All the inhabitants of Nkuma went running to Mbombe's house
635 To see what it was
"What is it?" asked Ilele and all the Nkuma people
"It is a fruit called *nsafu,*" responded Mbombe
"Boil it, put a bit of salt and I will eat it
It is a sweet fruit."
640 Spending days and nights without food
Had been a terrible experience for Mbombe
Her mind and soul now opened and her body leaped with joy
She was ready to receive more fruits from the calao
Which had already gone very far and for ever
645 At the break of the day, Mbombe sat down on the ground
And started to sing:
"Calao, calao, will you marry me
It is the calao which brought me food
Oh! calao... Oh Mother calao
650 Oh! Show my husband where to get more *nsafu* for me
Ilele my husband, feed me only with *nsafu.*"

The bird that was thought to have bad omen
Had brought food to the starving mother of the hero
The bird that was to be killed by the hunters of Nkuma
655 Was then invited to bring more fruits to the mother of the hero
When Mbombe sang, Ilele did not like her song
But he consoled her and showed her love
She sang again the same words to the bird
The whole Nkuma village heard her song
660 As it watched the evening glide under dark colours
But there was no calao in the sky
A firefly emerged from the top of a fig tree
At the far end of the village
But it could not fly like the proud and arrogant calao
665 That had brought food to the mother of the hero
The moon joined with the firefly
In lashing Nkuma with brighter lights
The whole village, mesmerised, went into a deep sleep
Mbombe was heard again early at dawn, singing the same words
670 Repeating the same words over and over
It was as though she was blaming those
Who had chosen her to be the hero's mother
After she had sobbed aloud her sorrow she fell asleep
Ilele then took over from her, singing:
675 "Calao, calao, come here with your loaded bill
Calao, calao, come with your big bill
Where did you find the *nsafu* you gave my wife?
Calao, calao, save my wife
Calao, calao, where can I get *nsafu*?
680 Mbombe, Mbombe my wife, would you like to marry a bird?
Mbombe, Mbombe my wife
Never look only at one side of the moon"
After Ilele had finished singing
He decided to go and look for *nsafu*
685 He did not know which way to take
Where had the two-billed bird come from?
The South, the East, the West or the North?
Ilele followed a path behind his house to a quiet forest
From there he went to the North of Nkuma Village
690 Crossed a river, then reached an abandoned village
He saw a shrine poised on two adjacent mountains
He knew, it was a place inhabited by the evil spirits

He went on his way very quietly
Holding three empty baskets in his hands
695 He jeered at all the efforts of the evil spirits
To destroy humankind
He knew he was in the region of the Sau-Sau
Satan's representatives on earth
Those whose duty it was to destroy *Ngiambe's* gifts
700 He was aware that if the Sau-Sau saw him in their territory
They would kill him
He therefore monitored closely their moods
He was suspicious and scared in the devil's land
The Mongo always remember, even today
705 How violently the Sau-Sau
Hate and kill them whenever they meet
Speaking to himself, Ilele silently said:
"I wonder why the Sau-Sau so bitterly hate the Mongo?
I wonder what causes the Fete-Fete and the Sau-Sau
710 To stand so firmly against the Mongo people?
Why do they gang up to destroy a whole ethnic group?
Why do they among the multitude of the ethnic groups
Pick on Mongo?
None of us has ever cast ill-natured words against them
715 Is it because we strongly believe in the power of creation?
We are convinced that whatever satanic strategem the evil spirits
May bring to us, the Mongo will survive
If they set out boldly to defend themselves
And believe in *Ngiambe's* promise
720 His words and those of the Ancestors
Shall make humankind stronger."
Ilele spoke silently to himself
The wilderness carefully listened to his thoughts
After he had walked a long distance
725 And after a moment of rest
He uttered to himself words of reconciliation
"We Mongo and the other tribes
Hated by the Sau-Sau and the Fete-Fete
Must all forgive them
730 For they do not know what they are doing
They are being misled by their masters, the evil spirits
By our action and love, we shall create peace in this cosmos
One day, all mankind shall be united

There will no longer be enemies
735   Of the living and the dead
The whole human race shall be reborn in a better form."
He remembered the promise of *Ngiambe*
He remembered a hero would be born from his wife Mbombe
To reconcile enemy tribes on the earth cosmos
740   And lead them to a land of peace and prosperity
As Ilele entered the thick forest of the Sau-Sau
He saw a tree full of *nsafu*
The fruit his wife so loved
But the tree full of *nsafu* belonged to Chief Sau-Sau
745   That tree was a taboo tree, and nobody could touch it
That tree was guarded by a leprous Fete-Fete
Whose wounds would never heal as a punishment from God
As Ilele went near the tree, the leprous Fete-Fete
Who was lying down on the ground
750   Stood up with his horrible wounds:
"Where are you going, you idiot animal?"
Asked the foul-smelling guard
"Don't you know that nobody is allowed to trespass
Upon Sau-Sau's property?"
755   Continued the stinking Fete-Fete
Ilele uttered not one word
He started to pluck some *nsafu*
"May leopards and cannibals eat you
Stinking and hopeless man
760   I challenge you and your master, the evil spirits
If you ever come near me again
I shall cut off your head," said Ilele
The leper had no choice but to call on other Sau-Sau
Though Ilele knew that his magic bell had been stolen
765   He did not lose his faith in *Ngiambe* and the Ancestors
He did not know that his wife Mbombe
Had put her own magic bell in one of the baskets
As he dropped the two baskets on the ground, the bell rang
He took it and saw that it was his wife's
770   When he shook the magic bell, thunder blew and the rain fell
The forest became very dark
Trees fell down and the guards died
Such a rain had never fallen before in the Sau-Sau land
Causing loss of people and property

775 As the hurricane was blowing down houses
And thunder destroying the forest
One Mongo who had betrayed his tribe and become a Sau-Sau ally
Returned to Nkuma
And entered Ilele's room while Mbombe was asleep
780 He searched everywhere but could not find Mbombe's magic bell
Since it was not in Ilele's house
He concluded that he had it with him
He went to the Chief Sau-Sau's house
To inform him about Ilele's magic bell
785 All the evil spirits came to the Sau-Sau Chief
They decided to summon the evil birds of the under-earth cosmos
And those in all the Sau-Sau villages to go and attack Ilele
Multitudes of birds flocked to the taboo tree
The most active and talkative was the sparrow-hawk
790 It sang: "Birds of the sky, come, come all of you
Come to protect the tree of our masters
Come, come, let us fight and kill the thief of our fruits
Come, come, let us slap him on the face
Come, come, may your wings make him blind
795 Come, come, let us not let him find his way back."
Ilelangonda saw all the birds and angry red eyes, ready to kill
A very strange red bird came, went around the tree five times
And began to sing: "I am the most powerful bird in the world
I know where Ilele's powers reside
800 Snatch the little bell from him
He will be like a child born today
Break the little bell he is holding
He will be like a child born today
Wait I shall snatch it from him
805 And you shall see
He will be like a child born today
Wait I shall dance my magic dance
And you will see
He will be like a child born today,"
810 Ilelangonda threw a *nsafu* at the bird
Then a second and third
The bird fell down but did not die and flew up again
Ilele continued to throw *nsafu* at it to kill it
But in vain
815 It was a mysterious bird with a very black tail

And a green bill, not seen before
The mysterious bird began to dance its magic dance
Then it flew away and was replaced by a wild canary
Which as soon as it reached the tree
820   Flew around it five times
A *nsafu* thrown by Ilelangonda hit it on the back
The wild bird stuck its bill into the tree
All the fruits thrown at it by Ilele did not touch it
The canary also looked very strange
825   With a black bill and yellow feathers
What was surprising was that
All these birds felt neither threatened nor frightened
After all the birds had arrived at the battle field
And after all the warriors had gathered around the taboo tree
830   A couple of peacocks arrived, flying with pride
At the rhythm and tune of the war drums
Beaten by the Sau-Sau
A second pair of peacocks arrived, determined to end the battle
Ilele did not waste time, he threw fruits at them
835   The peacock hit on the head and wings
Fell to the ground and died
Men, women, children, warriors and non-warriors
Were there around the tree watching
Ilele killed all the birds except the peahen which flew away
840   The Sau-Sau and the Fete-Fete met with the evil spirits
And decided to cut the tree
The chief evil spirit and Chief Sau-Sau endorsed the decision
For they were the commanders-in-chief
The peahen that survived turned its head from under its wing
845   And shared some secret words with Chief Sau-Sau
It seemed to say: "Once more I shall attack the thief and kill him."
Peafowls are loved by the other birds
They are also the most favourite of the evil spirits' birds
Often they are utilised for greater acts of boldness
850   They do not fight much
For they easily tear into pieces their opponents
The peahen again went up the tree
And faced Ilelangonda where he hid in the midst of the branches
The Sau-Sau, the Fete-Fete and the evil spirit watched
855   As Ilele angrily threw green *nsafu* at the peahen
It was a fierce combat of man against bird

The angry man was heard shouting:
"I will kill all the birds which belong to the evil spirits
I will kill them, all of them will die."
860 The green *nsafu* thrown at the peahen felt to the ground with a thud
A fire was lit under the taboo tree to burn it
Roaring cries of multitudes of evil spirits
The Sau-Sau and Fete-Fete from all over were heard
Chief Sau-Sau climbed to the top of a hill
865 To get a vantage point from which he could watch all the events
The beating, the striking, the shooting and the falling
He saw Ilelangonda pouring a rain of *nsafu* on the warriors' bird
Then from a distance, he saw the bird retreating to another tree
After a while, it again started its violent fight with Ilele
870 The bird multiplied its attacks on him
Slapped him on the face with its hard wings
The man lost control, his magic bell fell on the floor
The peahen gained momentum
Chopped Ilele's two eyes with its bill
875 Weakened, Ilelangonda staggered
Collapsing at the same spot where his magic bell had fallen
He began to utter his last words as great fighter and leader
Turned his face in an effort
To glance at the world for the last time
880 "Permit me, Great Ancestors, to join you
Let me come and sleep in peace where you are
I have fought a fierce fight with the servants of the Chief Devil."
Once again, he attempted to run in the direction of Nkuma
But his soul and strength departed and his body lay on the soil
885 The Sau-Sau, the Fete-Fete and the evil spirits rushed and cut off his head
Then they cut both hands and legs
Removed the lungs, the intestines, the heart and the pancreas
They cut the organs into very small pieces
Wrapped them up in wild leaves
890 And sent them to the Nkuma people, who were already aware
That their leader had been killed
They had heard the monkey in the forest cry
They had seen the snakes crawl to Nkuma
They had seen the elephants in the forest stand on the roads
895 There was blood pouring from the ceiling of Ilele's house
They heard the lions in the savannah roar
They saw minks running wildly in the bush

They heard the village cats miaow at daytime
Yes, the powerful Ilele was dead
900 Butchered by the Sau-Sau
The powerful Ilele who had fought in a pool of palm oil
The powerful Ilele who won the invincible Mbombe
Yes, Ilele was dead that day
And butchered by the Sau-Sau
905 The messenger who rushed to Nkuma to announce Ilele's death
Carried the parcel in which the pieces of the dead body were
He gave it to Mbombe herself, who first addressed the man and said:
"The Sau-Sau have killed my beloved husband because of *nsafu*
By this death, they think
910 They have won victory over the Nkuma Mongo!
It is not a victory
Their punishment is to come very soon
They will not be punished by the living Mongo
But by *Ngiambe* and the Ancestors."
915 One elder spoke up immediately
He did not like what Mbombe had said
For him, there and then, the Mongo should go
And avenge the death of their leader
He shouted:
920 "We have fought many wars with this band of ruffians
We must order all our warriors
To lift their shields and avenge Ilele
Nobody will remain behind this time
We shall exterminate them
925 And make slaves their children and women
This should be our last battle with them
For all of them must be killed
The Sau-Sau have stabbed our leader to death
We must revenge, otherwise they will never stop."
930 All the elders present were of the same opinion
But Mbombe restrained them saying:
"Give a chance to *Ngiambe* and the Ancestors
To teach the Sau-Sau a lesson
Killing and exterminating them is not the solution
935 Our warriors have enough enthusiasm
To win and wipe out the whole Sau-Sauland
The demise of these dishonest creatures will bring
Tears to generations to come
The problem will never be solved by hatred and revenge

940	Anger in the chests of righteous men never prevails
	The promised envoy of *Ngiambe* and the Ancestors
	Will be soon in our midst
	It is he who shall tell the Mongo how to resolve the problem
	Which has always existed between them and the Sau-Sau
945	Very soon, both the Mongo and the Sau-Sau will discover
	The truth of *Ngiambe's* creation
	For the time being, let us mourn our leader
	Let our love for those who hate us
	Soothe all the injuries in our souls."
950	As Mbombe finished speaking these words of wisdom
	Another messenger burst into the room
	Reporting that the Sau-Sau had kidnapped
	And assaulted a young Mongo girl
	Working in the field with her mother
955	The elders in the meeting room burst out like thunder
	They spat on the ground and swore by their honour
	To declare war on the Sau-Sau and the Fete-Fete
	An elderly man in the meeting stood and spoke to Mbombe:
	"Mbombe, you are the wife of our leader
960	Though you are not from Nkuma Village
	Have we not respected and shown you all our love and kindness?
	Have we not given you all the honour due to the wife of a leader?
	Why should you then condone the bandits' misconduct?
	Do not desecrate the Nkuma people's love for you
965	We must fight and die to protect our village
	The people of Nkuma have never been coward warriors
	We have never disgraced our Ancestors and our children
	We shall fight to protect our families and our land
	Never have we, or shall we
970	Tolerate acts of banditry and barbarism
	If we authorise our enemies to decimate our people
	If we allow thugs to assault and kidnap our daughter and wives
	Then this land no longer belongs to our Ancestral Forefathers
	We will have failed in our duty of protecting our land
975	The Sau-Sau claim their armies gain them reputation and honour
	We should therefore stop them by all means and at all costs
	When the elder finished speaking Mbombe, stood up
	And asked to respond:
	"I am a Nkuma woman, not a stranger at all
980	This land belongs to my father and Forefathers-in-law

It belongs to my deceased husband
It will belong to my children and the children of my children
Thus, it is my land by right
Only people with immaturity would think I am a stranger
85 Such people cannot be said to be different from the Sau-Sau
For they too are capable of committing heinous acts like the Sau-Sau
If the very custodians of public morals
Are the very ones who seek revenge
Then they are no longer bound
90 By the teachings of their *Ngiambe* and Ancestors
Go now and fight the Sau-Sau
I swear you will fight alone
No ancestor will be with you there
Because if you go, you also will show a lack of love
95 The Mongo people's minds should not be so warped
That they become unable to tell right from wrong
At this moment of crisis
Mongo people should show maturity
They need to strengthen their faith in *Ngiambe*
000 And wait for His will to be done in their land
What the Ancestors and *Ngiámbe* expect us to do now is simple:
Let us plead with them for protection and divine mercy
For us, our children, the children of our children and our land
The griots tell us that in ancient times
005 Our Forefathers never rushed to war
They thoroughly prepared, planned and conceived strategies
Even for a small battle
How can you decide to fight without preparation?
What is happening to us now is the work of the evil spirits
010 Because *Ngiambe* has allowed it to happen
Who are we to decide to change
The will of the Ancestors and *Ngiambe*?
Who told you they are not testing us to see how faithful we are?
Ngiambe and the Ancestors reveal their will to us very soon
015 Let us remain faithful at this moment of mourning."
Mbombe's words silenced all the elders in the room
Though they all respected her
They never knew she had such wisdom
By the power of her mind, Mbombe influenced the elders
020 To change their decision to go to war
They understood that should they go to war with the Sau-Sau

They and their children would die there
For *Ngiambe* would not be with them
They understood that they lived here on earth to acquire wisdom
1025   That would allow them to grasp the secret truth of life
And come to discover many other things unknown to mankind
They finally understood that by not avenging Ilele
They would cure many social evils
The same elder who before had spoken, stood up and said:
1030   "Mbombe, our very respected Lady
You are the wisest Lady we have ever had in our village
Your speech surpassed all others
I spoke in anger, I know
The Sau-Sau have spilled the blood of the Mongo
1035   Our families have been destroyed
Split because of their banditry
I thought you would concur with me
That the Sau-Sau are a nuisance to the Mongo people."
The Lady of Wisdom followed
1040   The elder's words with attention and interest
Knowing it was important to cool down tempers boiling
So she replied gently saying
"No Mpaka (elder, wiseman)! It is you the elders who are wiser
And greater than the other Nkuma people who rely on you
1045   I am very sure you know that it is wise
To avoid killing one's enemies
Certainly, no solution comes from violence or bloodshed
In our case, we need to ponder the matter
And then behave in accordance with Mongo ethics, customs and tradition
1050   Don't you know, sir
That through bloodshed, a whole generation may change its destiny
Power finds its strings in dialogue, love, peace and reconciliation."
Another elder, the youngest man in the meeting, requested to speak
He said: "I am thankful to *Ngiambe* for the love and mercy
1055   He has always shown to the Mongo people on the earth cosmos
We elders are here to fulfill the duties of our land
As requested by *Ngiambe*, the Ancestors and the living Mongo
We should remain loyal to them in any decision we take
In our conduct and in all the exercise of our duties
1060   I personally do not advocate war
As the highly respected wife of our Chief Ilelangonda has said
We need a time of peace and meditation upon the death of Ilelangonda

We need to dedicate ourselves to him
And concentrate on his funeral
)65 We need to prepare our souls and minds
For the hero's coming
After the youngest elder had spoken thus
The elders and Mbombe discussed how Ilele's death
Would be officially announced to the Mongo and their friends
)70 And how the traditional ceremonies of death would be conducted
Towards the end of the day, gongs and drums announcing Ilele's death
Were beaten by the elders and the griots of Nkuma
The sounds of drums and gongs travelled through all Mongoland
And went by their own power, beyond to neighbouring countries
)75 They sounded in the cosmos of the Ancestors and that of *Ngiambe*
Immediately, fearful cries of mourning
Exploded throughout the Ancestors's cosmos
Nkuma became dull and sad
No human being could believe the drums
)80 Nobody could believe that Ilelangonda was dead
Killed by the Sau-Sau
Nkuma people left their homes and settled at the mourning place
Thus started the greatest and longest mourning for Ilelangonda
Families, clans, tribes and sister countries
)85 Came to sympathise with the people of Nkuma
Never in the history of mankind had there ever been such mourning
Never in all legends about the cosmos of the Ancestors and Spirits
Had humankind been told of such sorrow and grief
Sadness inspired groups of griots and singers
)90 To compose poems of excellence
Which were either sung, recited, chanted or dramatised
Multitudes of mourners joined different groups of griots and singers
It was as though all the mourners were to die
And be buried along with Ilele
)95 It was as if life had suddenly left the cosmos of the earth
Everywhere, villages, cities, streets, roads and paths
Were so choked up with mourners
People wept, cried, shouted and called out Ilele's name
Mourners scattered to all visible and invisible lands:
100 The whole universe and the large group of stars
In which our own sun
And its planets lie, were shocked
And engulfed by one great seizure of grief and sadness

In the forests, animals also were seized by a long period of mourning
1105 The aquatic animals were choked up with strong emotion
Unable to express themselves
Birds sang sorrowful songs
While monkeys in the trees sighed in sadness
In all *Ngiambe's* creation, men and women
1110 Clustered together around fires and sang songs of mourning
That echoed from mountain to mountain
And conveyed the fierce message of a beloved chief's death
A voice shot through the ceremonial air of Nkuma
A female voice, that of Mbombe, Ilelangonda's wife
1115 She wept, her face painted in black
Her hair undone and her torso naked
She sprayed herself with white dust on the head and chest
Barefooted, she walked around the house
In which she had lived with Ilele
1120 Trying to imitate the way
Her dead husband had walked around
She wept, shouted and sang:
"Oh! death, voice of darkness and gloom
Which woman in this world is hit by so many misfortunes as Mbombe?
1125 Winds of evil spirits, why have you decided to blow on me?
Ilele my husband, where have you gone to? Come back Ilele!
Who will father the baby I am going to deliver soon?
Who shall it see first? Come and take me along with you!
Ilele my husband, which woman on earth has experienced so much sadness
1130 Ilele my husband, why did you decide to leave me alone."
Male mourners heard her and responded with another song:
"The death which has hit Nkuma is very fearful!
Ilele, the only male elephant of the Mongoland has ceased to be!
Mbombe, what will be the fate of the child you are going to bear!
1135 How will you rear him single-handedly
Who shall build the new house
In which you and your child will sleep?
Our land has become arid
Who will climb the palm trees
1140 To tap palm wine for you after you deliver your baby?
Who will fish for you?
Who will hunt for you?
Who will draw water for you
In your favourite calabash from Nkuma pool?

45 Nobody will go to the pool
For the Mongo and their friends are wailing with sorrow
Our songs of sorrow have risen high above the cliffs
Hills, mountains and valleys have dried up
They have become barren
50 In answer to our mourning songs
Mbombe who will hear you? Who will see you? Who will console you?
Mbombe, you have become a lonely woman
Who will provide you with human warmth and male perfume?
The earth's eyes can no longer see
55 Its warmth can no longer be felt
Life in our cosmos has come to an end
Our cosmos has become inert like a rock in the River Zaire
Yes, Ilele's death has forced him and the Mongo asunder
Yes, it has created two different worlds:
60 Where he is now and where we have remained
Yes, Ilele has gone to the Ancestors
What did he leave for us, for our children
For the children of our children?
Yes, Ilelangonda will be remembered for centuries and centuries
65 Ilele has set a good example of leadership for future generations."
A group of women in black clothes
Who were sitting on the ground replied:
"What voice are we hearing? Is that the voice of death
Which has taken away our Patriarch Ilelangonda?
70 Do you mean death wants to turn Mongoland
Into a gloomy wilderness?
Should we flee and abandon our fertile land
Because of the Sau-Sau's violence?
Never! Mongo people will never wander the forest
75 We shall remain in the village built by our husbands
When it rains and night falls
We shall find shelter in our huts
We shall light the fire of family communion and love in our huts
We shall live in the village of our Ancestral Forefathers
80 When the sky is covered with dark clouds
We shall find refuge in our huts right here in Nkuma
Oh! death, you have carried the body of our Patriarch
You have let loose the dogs and hyenas
Which eat human flesh and laugh
85 They have killed our Patriarch, Mbombe's beloved husband

71

And left her without a man to plough
To cut big trees in the fields
Oh! death, you are the voice of the evil-spirits
Which dwell under earth
1190 What size are you?
What shape are you?
Are you round like the earth?
Bordered by North, South, East and West?
With whom do you share the many human bodies
1195 You carry away every minute?
Tell us, death, what do you do with our people?"
A group of young girls stood under the baobab tree
Where Ilele had always rested
They carried mourning gifts
1200 Which they gave to Mbombe, their Lady of Wisdom.
They sat on the ground, sobbed and lamented
for their departed Patriarch:
"Let us lament with a sad voice
That can be heard in the whole cosmos
1205 Let our voice be heard by the Patriarch where he is
Let our voice bring back our Patriarch from where he is
Let the people of the whole world fight
For our Patriarch to come back here to Nkuma
Let people of the world become deaf so they cannot hear
1210 Blind so they can not see
The barbaric and criminal acts of the Sau-Sau
Is it not despicable of the Sau-Sau
To have killed a Mongo leader of such high esteem?
Let us sing, build a holy house so that the sanctity of our nakedness
1215 And the secrets of our Forefathers can be hidden and sealed in it
Let young generations hide our thoughts from the Sau-Sau
May heaven descend on us and take us away
From this cosmos of wickedness
Heavens, come, come and take us away, we do not want to suffer
1220 May black insects invade our cosmos
So that we all die like our Patriarch
Earth and heaven, stop breeding wicked men and women
Earth and heaven, let the Sau-Sau escape with our sorrow
Heaven and earth have met today to unite under one leadership
1225 Nations have united today to create one big and powerful nation.
Today heaven and earth have shed tears never shed before

Today nations have experienced grief not experienced before
Mountains and hills have witnessed the sadness of nations
Rivers and forests have witnessed the misfortune of our nations."
230   Mbombe joined the group of widows sitting in the parlour
They sang laments no human being had ever sung before
Their heads shook and their bodies trembled like leaves as they wept
The refrain of their laments ran like this:
"Rivers, lakes and oceans, pour water on us, for Ilele is dead
235   Trees in the forests fall down, for Ilele is dead
Monkeys in the trees and elephants, cry, weep, for Ilele is dead
Our Patriarch, the man who was protecting you is dead."
Mbombe lamented in a deep and sad voice
That made her gorge rise
240   The drums were still beating and the trumpet blowing
Sending news about Ilele's death to the whole globe
The sun opened its eyes
It was a day with long eyelashes
That cleared up the skies and heavens
245   The day was born, a day of bitterness and sorrow
The mourners went on singing, sobbing, lamenting and chanting
Their songs, sobs, laments and chants
Sung with tears and deep voices of sadness
Created a cacophony of discordant sounds
250   The blind and crippled mourners sat together
Playing different musical instruments
They warned: "Let us remain faithful to the Mongo traditions
Let us not bring another calamity to our home
Because of disrespect for tradition
255   Women, do not touch your hoes during the mourning period
Do not put your hoes on your shoulders
Blacksmiths, stop forging the iron
Listen to the griots who mourn
Palm-wine tapsters, do not climb the tree in the evening
260   Do it in the morning
Palm-wine tapsters, bring your calabashes of wine to the mourning place
Let your sweet palm wine soothe the mourners' sore throats
Young girls and boys, forget about marriage during this time
May all the unmarried boys and girls remain single
265   May all the grounds remain untilled and abandoned
May all the fields be full of grass
May paths disappear in the mountains, hills, valleys and forests

73

Let nobody travel during this time of mourning."
Mbombe's relatives remained behind the house in the open air
1270 They wept bitterly and mourned for their in-law
"Why should we not weep?
Why should we not tear our clothes?
The one who bought them for us is dead
Day and night, we shall weep and shout the name of Ilele
1275 It is because of the love he had for Mbombe
That our in-law died
Why then should we not remember him?
O! death, we shall not see
Again our brother and son-in-law
1280 The sun shall not again
Shed its soft light on our Patriarch
Ilele, our son and brother
We won't say goodbye, but just *au revoir*
For you have gone to a place we cannot yet reach
1285 You shall not come again to a land under the sun
Brothers and sisters, Ilele won't laugh again with us
Ilele won't sit again on his throne
He has gone to enjoy his great moment of joy and happiness."
In the afternoon of the day
1290 That followed the assassination of Ilele
The people of Nkuma buried the small pieces of his body
Sent to Mbombe by the Sau-Sau
Fearful was the occasion of Ilele's burial
More fierce dirges of burial burst forth
1295 From the crowds at the cemetery
Congregations of men and women sang the last burial song
Then Mbombe took a fistful of soil in her right hand
Threw it into the grave and onto the coffin
Uttering her last words to her departed husband
1300 She was weak and sad for she had not eaten for weeks
Two women held her from the left and from the right
For she had no strength left in her
Being pregnant, she should not have had to mourn her husband
But what Mongo woman would not mourn her dear husband?
1305 Mbombe started to speak in a shaky voice:
"Ilele my husband
You are gone. Who did you leave me with?
You should not have gone. You should have pitied me!
You have left me pregnant!"

74

1310   Then she started to shout aloud the name of Ilele
        As though she had gone insane
        The gathering at the cemetery started to weep and cry
        After she had recollected herself
        She narrated how she lived happily with their husband
1315   How she became pregnant and refused to eat food
        How the calao bird came and dropped the *nsafu*
        That she boiled and ate with appetite
        How Ilele fought the first time with the Sau-Sau, the Fete-Fete
        And the evil-spirits whom he easily defeated
1320   She told the mourners at the cemetery how famine started to hit Nkuma
        How the elders and counsellors met the last time with Ilele
        And what they discussed during their last meeting with him
        She also told the crowd how Ilele fought the second fight
        Against the birds that he killed one by one
1325   Until a couple of peacocks arrived at the taboo tree
        How the female peacock had attacked Ilele and gouged out his eyes
        How his magic bell had fallen down and he too fell later on the same spot
        She repeated to the mourners the very last word Ilelangoda her husband
        Had uttered before his soul departed from the body
1330   After she had finished narrating these events, episode by episode
        The eldest of the elders spoke on behalf of all the mourners
        Because of the sadness of the occasion, the elder had lost his elequence
        He spoke in a staccato voice, gasping irregularly
        He cleared his throat several times with his own saliva
1335   Then he too, took a handful of soil in his right hand
        And held it while speaking:
        "Ilele our Patriarch, on behalf of all present here
        I beg you to listen to our last conversation with you
        You have gone to a place
1340   Where our minds cannot comprehend
        Where you are now
        Only the Spirits and our Ancestors can talk to you
        As from the time you departed
        We became unworthy to talk with you
1345   But please, today lend us your ears and listen to us
        Wherever you are, please intercede for us
        So that *Ngiambe* and our Ancestors continue to help us
        Let them continue to provide us with their sacred brotherhood
        Let them continue to offer us wisdom
1350   To grasp our alliance with them

You knew in your life-time many secrets
And you acquired knowledge
Which we think we need for the enhancement and the fulfilment
Of our duties here on earth
1355   Please send them back to us
Teach us those techniques
And give us those weapons for fighting the evil-spirits."
The elder spoke to Ilelangonda as though he were still alive
For it is not uncommon among the Mongo
1360   To address the dead as if they were alive
Though they have passed from this world to a better one
They interact with us in all our activities here on earth
After the eldest elder had spoken thus to Ilele
Groups of mourners sang farewell songs to the deceased Patriarch
1365   Each group sought to be the best one at singing and mourning
Then the mourners retreated, starting with Mbombe and her relatives
It was as if mourners were angry with one another
And this sorrow was not over
After they had washed their hands
1370   The mourners wept again
Death had cut the nights and days of joy
That the Mongo people were proud of
Late in the afternoon of the burial day
When sunbeams disappeared behind the tall trees
1375   The great anthem of the Mongo people and friends
Filled the air of Nkuma
As Mbombe sat with other women
The mourning songs started again
Groups of mourners formed themselves independently
1380   This time, the men kept silent, but some of them
Delegates from different nations and clans
Were introduced to the crowd
Before the night had covered the earth
Cows, bulls, goats and chickens
1385   Were slaughtered and cooked
Numbers of clans offered foodstuffs
Beverages, liquor, kegs of palm wine
To feed the Mongo and visiting mourners who were present
There was enough food to be eaten during the whole period of mourning
1390   After evening meals, the mourners returned to their places
Where palm-wine and other types of local beverages

Were served to them
After they had eaten and drunk
Different bands and orchestras played music
1395 And the people celebrated and danced at the mourning place
For it is believed
It is during the time of celebration and dance
That the poets compose poems of praise
During these times
1400 The griots and orchestra sing the greatness of the deceased
They sing the anthems of various heroes of the tribe
And other mourners watch in silence with tears in their eyes
The evening after Ilele's burial
Great numbers of decorated mourners filled the compound:
1405 All the dignitaries, councillors and guests
Mingled together with the ordinary people
Among those who could be seen were rulers of guest countries
Who came in big delegations of men, women and children.
Each delegation carried their anthems and shields
1410 A great silence reigned in the crowds
As they waited for Mbombe
Her face and feet were being washed
And she was to be dressed
By five old women, who were her aides
1415 The heads of the crowd moved inquisitively from right to left
Like waves in the River Zaire when blown by a storm
Five male aides announced Mbombe's arrival
The five female aides circled her
While the males protected her
1420 She was adorned with black bracelets
And other traditional ornaments of black colour
She was led to where other widows were
She sat with them for she had joined them forever
She was joined by her mother, sisters and female cousins
1425 Who also were dressed completely in black
Those who were closer to Ilele wept for a moment
But they were told to stop weeping
For that was the time men had to debate
The future of the widow
1430 They had to take care of her
Otherwise the deceased husband
Would inflict calamity on the living
For having neglected his wife

77

THIRD NIGHT

THE BIRTH OF THE HERO

After several months of mourning
The people's bitterness turned into love
The people of Mongo still went to visit Mbombe in Nkuma
They arrived from distant places
5   With their gifts to the widow
Some came from as far as Lodja
Driving herds of goats, cows and sheep
Others arrived from as far as Mudongoland and its environs
They all went again to Nkuma after the mourning period
10   For a courtesy visit and gift-giving ceremony
On this occasion Mbombe's compound was full of people
And herds of animals
It was noisy and full of activity
The hunting dogs of Nkuma were jealous
15   They wondered why humankind
Never shared equally with them
The meat of the animals they protected and reared together
They had hoped Mbombe would give them
At least half of the animals
20   But great was their disappointment
Any time one of them barked
Or just happened to pass by Mbombe's compound
Stones were thrown at them
In desperation, they retreated
25   And went for the bones of the animals killed during the funeral
All *Ngiambe's* creatures in the land of Lukundo were happy again
The rivers, lakes, oceans filled up with water and fish
Trees in the forest grew back their green leaves
Animals stampeded and savoured the green forest grass
30   Birds filled the Nkuma skies and sang melodiously in the tree tops
Giraffe and zebra gave birth to new young
Hyenas, lions, leopards and cheetahs gave thanks to *Ngiambe*
For there was plenty of food to eat and water to drink
Women in the villages screamed with joy to *Ngiambe*
35   They were able to feed their husbands and children
Young boys who were trained to be professional hunters
Graduated easily, for there were many beasts to kill

78

Young fishermen went alone to the rivers
Leaving their masters at the village
40   For there were plenty fish in the rivers
In the savannahs warthogs could roll on the grass and eat it
Sit on it, run fast and free
Throw themselves in the air
Leap up towards the skies
45   As though they had triumphed over nature
With all its calamities
When the neighbouring Sau-Sau and the Fete-Fete heard
And saw the herds of animals cursing them
They would hide in the valley
50   And try to shoot or trap them
But none would be killed nor wounded
Instead, the herds of beasts decimated
And devoured thousands of Sau-Sau hunters
Animals organized themselves into armies according to their species
55   The elephants, the cheetahs, the lions, tigers and leopards
Formed a powerful regiment
War was declared between the Mongo animals and the Sau-Sau
The elephants were the first to attack the Sau-Sau army of hunters
The lions and hyenas followed
60   Eating the flesh of the hunters killed by the elephants
Screeching with pain, the fleeing hunters cried out:
"Leave us alone! you Mongo animals."
On hearing the cries of dying Sau-Sau hunters
The evil spirits sent their own warriors and hunters
65   But the Mongo herds of animals did not retreat
They confronted the different regiments and pursued them
In total commotion, the evil spirits disappeared
To nobody knows where
Some griots say they were killed by the animals
70   Others believe they turned into rocks and were thrown into water
But whatever became of them
The Mongo animals had made one mistake
They had killed only the warriors
And mature males of the land of Sau-Sau and the evil spirits
75   Leaving the women and young boys and girls
When these young Sau-Sau and the evil spirits grew up
They became more evil than their deceased fathers
And so the problem between the Sau-Sau and the Mongo was never solved

Generation after generation of the Sau-Sau
80 The Fete-Fete and the evil spirits
Were born and grew up with hatred and hostility
The evil spirit race is said to multiply faster than mankind
In their land there is endless hardship
Because the land is arid and desert like
85 It is burnt up every day
By the mouths of the evil spirits which spit fire
And can burn vast areas of forests and valleys
There is great famine there
Suffering, prostitution, murder and crime
90 People cry all the time, lament their suffering
But their conditions never change
That is their fate because they broke *Ngiambe's* law
These are the evil spirits,
Who had conquered the Sau-Sau
95 Their Chief had given them an order:
To hunt for more followers
To enlarge their evil kingdom
"The Mongo people are stubborn and skeptical
To the reality of my truth," said the chief evil spirit
100 "I shall do my best to continue inflicting them with calamities
That will wipe them out
Their territory shall belong to my people, the Sau-Sau
They say they would remain faithful to their *Ngiambe* and Ancestors
But do they not know my powers equal those of their *Ngiambe?*
105 My people, the Sau-Sau, have butchered Ilelangonda
One of their greatest leaders
Why did not their *Ngiambe* and Ancestors protect him?
Well! they sent herds and herds of animals to attack our fathers
Why didn't their masters, the Mongo fight with our fathers?
110 Is it not because their *Ngiambe* and Ancestors
Knew that the Mongo would be defeated as usual!
Now, I the chief evil spirit, have sworn
To brutally ravage and attack all the Mongo villages
We shall burn and destroy them
115 Towns, cities and centres
I shall dwell in their Patriarch's palace
Extend my kingdom and power through the whole of Mongoland
I shall personally terrorize those who resist my warriors
I shall harass any man, woman or child

20   Who is called Mongo
The Sau-Sau and the Fete-Fete shall enjoy
The privileges of belonging to me
All Mongo families and clans will collapse and disappear at once."
The Sau-Sau the Fete-Fete and the evil spirits held many meetings,
25   Plotting the downfall of *Ngiambe* and the Ancestors
Why should the Mongo on earth cosmos
Live a decent and easy life while they suffered?
Their ultimate aim was
To make *Ngiambe's* rule over Mongo crumble
30   The chief evil spirit urged his people
To earnestly seek rule over all the different cosmos
He was consumed by the desire to rule the whole world
He surrounded himself with the wisest and most intelligent devils
Whom he appointed as strategists and advisors
35   To defeat *Ngiambe* and his people
But *Ngiambe's* intelligence surpasses that of the creature
Moulded by his own hand
Who knew what plan *Ngiambe* had for Mongo people?
The Ancestors, aware of the evil spirits' plan
40   Sent a delegation to *Ngiambe's* cosmos
Where they met for many hours with *Ngiambe*
They told Him: "Can't you see the evil spirits are disturbing the Mongo?
His people the Sau-Sau have already killed Ilele who is now with us
In the cosmos of the Ancestors
45   They are preparing to destroy the creatures
Placed by yourself on the earth cosmos
Their ambition is to rule the whole world
They have always fought for the downfall of your rule
Death is their weapon to cause deep pain to your creatures
50   Please help us to stop this insanity."
Ngiambe listened carefully, though He had seen
And knew what was happening
He said: "Rest assured that your *Ngiambe* knows
And sees everything everywhere
55   The evil spirits are not becoming insane
They are what they have always been
But they will do nothing to my people without my permission
They boast of having conquered the Sau-Sau and the Fete-Fete
But for how long?
60   They will soon abandon those evil spirits

To live in unity with the Mongo
I have heard you, I have heard too the Mongo people's prayer
Go, wait for my answer to you and to them, wait in faith."
Those griots who still live today
165 Tell us that when the delegation of Ancestors was talking to *Ngiambe*
They knelt down in front of Him
For He is the King of Kings
He was there before the beginning of time
He sees every creature He made in His image
170 Assured of *Ngiambe's* promise, the Ancestors descended to their own cosmos
Where they assembled all the male, female and children Spirits
The delegates informed them of the promise of *Ngiambe*, the Creator
Decades and decades passed and Mbombe was still pregnant
She kept on calling the name of *Ngiambe* and that of the Ancestors
175 She went on invoking them and seeking *Ngiambe's* divine protection
Sometimes she lost hope and thought she was carrying a monster
But her faith in *Ngiambe* grew and she believed and trusted in Him
"I have lived gazing at *Ngiambe's* wonders
I have longed to know, through these wonders who *Ngiambe* is
180 My desires have been fulfilled according to *Ngiambe's* will
I yearn to return home
Where *Ngiambe* and the Ancestors reside
Because of *Ngiambe's* love for me
Because of the many wonders *Ngiambe* had done for me
185 I shall always punctuate my faith in Him
With good actions to my fellow human beings
I thank *Ngiambe* again for choosing me among Mongo women
To bear for many years in my womb the hero of His people
I shall never fail to treasure
190 *Ngiambe's* desires and promises
I thank Him, I thank the Ancestors
I thank our Forefathers
Who have till now protected
And given us the wisdom we need
195 To resist the evil-spirits' persuasion
I thank Him for He has used me to perpetuate creation
I thank Him for He has through me
Enriched the life of mankind
I thank *Ngiambe* for the joy
200 I have experienced these last days
I thank *Ngiambe* for the grief and hardship

I have endured these last days
I shall always believe and trust in Him."
After this poem in praise of *Ngiambe*
205 The Creator of visible and invisible creatures
Mbombe felt she was transformed into a new being
She felt a new beginning in her life
She felt enlightened and enriched with new life
She knew the hero was about to be born
210 Though her body became comatose
She did not lose her mind
She knew what was happening to her body
One day, she suddenly gave birth
To billions and billions of ants
215 Some were white, others were red
Others yet, were black
Some were big, some were small
All those species of ants were voracious
They appeared unendingly like a concourse of bees
220 As soon as they appeared, they went into the forest
Where they terrified old boars, which with their snouts
Were busy cutting the roots of young trees
They also dismissed a herd of beasts
Meeting at the tree trunk of life and death
225 After the ants, varieties of insects appeared from Mbombe's womb
As never seen before in this world
They too took the same direction as the ants
Some flew into the skies, others spread in the trees
Mbombe was already tired
230 The ants and the insects continued to appear for many hours
But how could she be tired after labour pains of a day?
The task of procreation assigned to her by *Ngiambe* had just commenced
No sooner had she taken a rest
Than birds of all colours and types appeared
235 Some were big and others as tiny as the insects or ants
They too went into the forests, rivers, bushes and valleys
The women in the labour room were so amazed that some fled
But the more courageous remained to watch the miraculous births
To Mbombe's amazement, the insects were followed by human beings:
240 Skinny, sickly, weak, strong, ugly, beautiful
They appeared one after the other and assembled in Nkuma
They started gambolling around the huts and houses of Nkuma

They were hairy and shaggy like monkeys in the equatorial forest
After they had gambolled around the houses and huts of Nkuma
245   They all sang their birth anthem:
"We who are born today are the creatures of *Ngiambe*
We who are born today are the outcome of *Ngiambe*'s creation
We who are born today are the manifestation of Mongo heroism
Though we are small, we shall populate this land of *Ngiambe*
250   Tall, short, big, powerful or weak
We all are the outcome of His creation
We have to stop the destruction
Of the Mongo people by the evil spirits
We are issued from a lady Spirit
255   Who is the mother of the whole of mankind
She is our mother too
She was chosen by *Ngiambe* to perpetuate His creation
Why should the whole of humankind be destroyed
By the Sau-Sau and the Fete-Fete?
260   We are singing in our capacity
As the true great sons of Lukundo."
Throughout Mongoland, the news was heard
About Mbombe's delivery of various creatures
People flocked again to Nkuma to see
265   With their own eyes what was happening
Men, women and children rushed to Nkuma
Eager to see the creatures born of Mbombe
Through the rivers and oceans the aquatic animals went to Nkuma
Through paths of mountains, forests and valleys, the animals went to Nkuma
270   Through roads and routes, human beings of all social classes rushed to
Nkuma
They all converged in Nkuma
And mingled freely with each other
In the village of great miracles
Men travelled very fast to Nkuma
275   Leaving behind their wives and children
Women left their houses and dishes unwashed to rush to Nkuma
They left their cassava roots in water to rush to Nkuma
Some remembered to carry gifts for the mother and the new borns
Others forgot this tradition, especially the young women
280   Very seldom do the Mongo old forget their traditions!
They knew that however big their hurry
They had to carry at least a gift of food

Some of them carried cowries, lotion, money and clothes
Others carried quantities of grain, machetes, ploughs and hoes
285 Some brought gifts of male and female pets, goats and sheep
Others brought kegs of palm-wine
And big containers of locally brewed beer
Some came with diamonds and gold of the best quality
Others brought legs of roasted wild animals and dried fish
290 After Mbombe had delivered the skinny human beings
Her womb gave forth hunters and fishermen
Complete with their fishing and hunting tools
They were tall and huge
The muscles of their arms were strong as iron
295 They looked arrogant because of their physical strength
And seemed not at all interested in the world they had come to
They never looked at the Nkuma people
Nor did they talk with them
As soon as they appeared from Mbombe's womb
300 Some went towards the forest
Some took the direction of the rivers
And others followed the paths to the mountains and valleys
Who among those who were already born, was the hero?
Nobody knew!
305 Mbombe's womb was emptied of everything that was in it
"Has she stopped delivering human beings?
But where is the promised saviour?
Has he refused to come?
How can that be?" sighed the audience
310 Though the hero was not born
They had to respect the Mongo tradition
That after the birth of any child
People socialize, drink, dance, sing and eat
The men of Nkuma sat on their wooden chairs in Mbombe's compound
315 Young boys rushed back home to collect their musical instruments
Drums announcing the end of birth were beaten
Horns to salute and welcome the newborns were blown
The singers composed and sang songs to the newborns
While the bards of Nkuma narrated the legends of their Forefathers
320 Hunters narrated the most fascinating stories of their careers
Fishermen eulogized their skills and qualities
Women formed a circle, and sang of Mbombe's strength and courage
They danced and re-enacted the miraculous birth

Poems and cantatas were shouted from all corners of Nkuma
325 They were dedicated to *Ngiambe* and to the Ancestors
Thanking them for keeping Mbombe safe
And for bringing forth more creatures
Through the Wise Lady of Nkuma
The first person to begin the dance was an old man
330 Who lived alone, without a wife or child, in Nkolobeke town
Those griots who have lived still narrate today
How he killed ten leopards in his youth
He was, in fact, the man most feared by the Sau-Sau
He was renowned for killing elephants and other beasts bare handed
335 He went into battle without any weapon
And went hunting without a gun, bow or arrow
The old Nkolobeke man could plunge into water and remain there
For as long as he desired to live with the aquatic animals
As he started to dance
340 A terrible noise, like a thunder bolt, was heard from the sky
The noise was heard five times and struck the gathering with dismay
Many wondered fearfully what had happened again in Nkuma!
In whispers, some claimed
They were being attacked by the barbarian Sau-Sau
345 It was amidst this fear and commotion in Nkuma
That a virile voice was heard from the labour-room
Where Mbombe had been resting, with three midwives attending to her
Poor woman, she was tired and thought it was all over
The voice came from Mbombe's knee and said forcefully:
350 "Oh! mother, do not be tired for I am coming soon
Those who arrived before me announced my appearance
They are the premonitory signs of my triumphant appearance
They came before me as messengers to confirm my arrival
It is my turn now, I am not coming alone
355 I will come with my younger sister
Mother, get prepared to welcome your children
Please mother, follow my advice and keep your courage."
No sooner had the hero finished speaking
Than Mbombe's leg became as big as a baobab tree
360 The voice from the swollen knee
Was heard again for the second time:
"Mother, please do what I am going to tell you
You midwives attending to my mother
Obey my instructions to you:

365 Apply *kaolin* oil on my mother's right leg
Mother, apply kaolin oil on your right leg
Let it be wet completely with kaolin oil
Pour it mainly on the front of your right leg
Because I shall come through the knee
370 For I cannot take the way of the other creatures
I need a new way to come through
A way that is made only for me."
Terrified, those who were not aware
Of the advent of the hero's birth
375 Fled with their children and wives
As though they had heard a ghost talk
Nkuma was stricken by complete silence
The animals and the aquatic creatures
Were the second group to flee in terror
380 They were followed by the dogs and cats of Nkuma
Suddenly, the midwives' voices broke the silence and fear
They sang in response to the command given by the hero:
"Let us apply kaolin oil on Mbombe's leg
Let us get ready, our messiah is coming
385 Let us prepare our souls for his coming
May he come, our saviour!
May he come, our liberator!
May he come, our greatest hero!
With warmth and traditional Mongo hospitality
390 We shall welcome him
With all respect due to him
We shall bow our heads before him."
The midwives' voices echoed through the mountains and forests
Upon hearing the singing
395 The fleeing cowards came back to Nkuma
The multitude of people
Planted their feet on the ground
Like the roots of old trees which have penetrated the inner soil
They fixed their feet like roots because the earth shook
400 The trees and plants of Nkuma trembled to welcome the hero
A breeze wailed in the chimneys all day
Birds in the trees sang melodiously
While mountains and valleys opened up themselves to Nkuma
In gratitude for the Mongo people
405 The midwives' response to the hero's voice spread joy and happiness

In the hearts of all mankind
For the hero's birth was a historic event
People now wanted to reap the fruit of their patience
Of their suffering at the hands of the Sau Sau
410   Many had died without seeing the hero
Weak and tired of waiting so long
But the courageous Mongo endured the pain of waiting
The faithful survived while the weak died a spiritual death
Those who had sown their faith in *Ngiambe*
415   Now reaped the fruits of faithfulness
The thunder clouds of heaven came nearer and nearer
As if they would fall to the floor of Nkuma with a thud
They descended and settled in quietly for three hours
Then they rose and spread over the skies of Nkuma
420   From which a voice called out:
"Mbombe, Mbombe, the hero is about to come
Thou shalt name him LIANJA as the oracles
And the Spirit prophesied
Thy obedience to *Ngiambe* and to the Ancestors
425   Is without precedent
Thou shalt be remembered for ever
In all the cosmos of the living and the dead
For thou hast set a good example
To all women and men under the galaxy
430   Thou art a better woman
For thou has grown in wisdom and courage
And thou shalt be ever near *Ngiambe* and the Ancestors
Thou did not disobey the commands
Ngiambe gave the Mongo people
435   Thou cannot be forgotten
Either by human beings or by the Spirits
Behold, the son of Ilele is coming to earth with his two natures."
The voice was round and nobody saw the person speaking
As the voice stopped, Mbombe's knee swelled again
440   Around the knee, between the femur, the tibia and the patella
Appeared a red swelling which grew bigger and bigger
The whole leg became as huge as an elephant
Suddenly, water gushed forth from the swelling
It opened wide, and without any effort from Mbombe
445   A full grown man, very handsome, came from the open swelling
It was him, Lianja, who mankind had been waiting for

He appeared with all his war implements
All of them magical
Because Lianja was a spirit
450 On his left hand, he carried twelve arrows, a spear and a bow
On his right hand, he had one long knife and two machetes
He had on his head a hat made of leopard's skin
Ornamented with different accessories
He was wearing a green tunic
455 That he tied with a magic belt around his hips
A magic bell hung from it
His feet were big and bare
After some minutes, his sister Nsongo appeared
She also, was very beautiful
460 Indeed, the most beautiful girl on this earth
She was slender, with a fresh, soft and youngish skin
No sign of roughness or wrinkles on her jovial face
Lianja took her by the right hand and they both flew away
To go and inspect their father's country
465 "Follow me and let us visit our relatives and neighbours
Come, let us visit this country which is ours
Let us visit our neighbours who are also our relatives
Then, let us settle here in Nkuma with our people."
After inspecting their father's country
470 After they had encountered the spirits in the skies
They came back and landed on the roof of Mbombe's house
Great crowds and processions witnessed their return
Welcomed them back warmly
As they landed on the roof of Mbombe's house
475 Mbombe addressed them in these terms:
"Son Lianja and daughter Nsongo
This land of your father and forefathers welcomes you today
Lianja my son, the world has been awaiting your birth for many years
It is time you started to accomplish the mission
480 For which Ngiambe, the Ancestors and the Spirits have sent you
Do not wait
Mongoland has sunk into gloom, desperation and chaos
Our enemies the Sau-Sau, the evil spirits and the Fete-Fete
Are against your birth to the Mongo people
485 I know they know that you are already born
And some of these enemies are here in our midst
Soon they will retreat to go and plot against you

From where you are standing
On the roof of the house built by your father
490 Take the leadership of your brothers, sisters
And the entire community
Talk my son, address those who love you
They have come to greet you."
After Mbombe's address, Lianja and Nsongo came down from the roof
495 There they were, talking freely with everybody in the crowd
All wanted to shake hands with them, especially with Lianja
For they knew he was the redeemer of the whole world
The most powerful person sent by *Ngiambe* to save mankind
He was admired, worshipped and adored by all creatures
500 From all species, races, ethnic groups, countries
Tribes, villages, clans and families
Gongs and drums announcing the good news
Of the hero's birth were beaten
People danced and rejoiced, but they wanted to hear Lianja's address
505 They had heard the mother speak, but what about Nsongo and Lianja
Why did the mother speak before Nsongo and Lianja?
It is not normal for the mother to talk before her children
Mbombe was a great heroine for mankind
Her fame will remain eternal as once said the voice from the skies
510 She will shine on like the moon, the stars and the sun
Whoever has been told the story of Lianja wherever he is, always says:
"It is a pride and privilege to hear about the Mongo hero
Who reconciled tribes and ethnic groups."
But in the midst of the celebrations
515 Rejoicing, dancing and singing
A strange thought was nagging at the hero's soul and mind
He saw everybody, shook hands with them: men, women and children
He met his uncles, aunts, brothers and sisters
Though he had just come to a new life, Lianja knew who was who
520 His mother and the counsellors had introduced everybody to him
In her address, Mbombe passed over softly like a wind
The issue of the whereabouts of the hero's father
Her own husband, killed by the Sau-Sau
From where Lianja was sitting
525 He heard the voice of the people
Among whom he was going to live
He heard the songs often sung by the Spirits in their cosmos
He saw again the house he had lived in the spirit world

He thought he was dreaming but he was awake
530   Then a voice told him to ask where his father was
He stood up and went near his mother
Who was seated with other women
"Mother, mother, may I ask you a question?" the hero said
"Yes of course my son
535   I shall answer any question you will ask." replied Mbombe
Without knowing that the absence of Ilelangonda had disturbed the hero child
"Mother, where is my father? Your husband?
Where is my father? Why is he absent here today?
I want to see him, talk with him like I am talking with you."
540   That was a very embarrassing question for Mbombe
She had known that her son would want to know about his father
But did not expect him to do so on the very day he was born
She wondered what the hero's reaction would be
If truth was told to him
545   After all, he was only a few hours old
The mother did not know him much
She could not predict any reaction from the hero just born
She thought of calling a meeting of the elders and counsellors
During which the hero would be told diplomatically
550   About his father's death
She thought of dismissing the question
But she realized her son was very impatient
She was silent for a while
Then big drops of tears fell from her eyes
555   Mbombe's abrupt sadness surprised the new-born
He felt sick at heart and he left her alone
He did not know what had happened to his father
Nobody would tell him, even from the Spirit world he came from
"Did my father die?
560   If he did, who killed him?
Why is it difficult for all these people to tell me?
Are they waiting for an opportunity to do so?
And if so, which one?
Why did my mother not mention it in her welcome speech?"
565   These were the questions the hero asked himself
On his first day in this world
Because of his mother's sadness, he came to realize
That certainly his father was not alive
If he was, Lianja would have seen him

570   And his mother would not have wept
       "But how did he die?
       Of disease? Killed by the Sau-Sau?"
       At this precise time, Lianja began to understand
       The world he had come to live in
575   While he was battling with his strange thoughts
       Mbombe was sobbing silently
       While the crowd was rejoicing
       People divided into small groups of dancers and singers
       And sang: "We have seen for ourselves the long awaited Saviour
580   We have come to hear the great news of our hero's birth
       We have come to see Nsongo and Lianja
       Born of the Wise Lady
       From our Saviour, we shall learn the truth of our life
       Our Saviour shall feed our minds and souls
585   With the secrets of life
       We shall sing to honour *Ngiambe*
       The Ancestors and our Saviour."
       Somebody in one of the groups
       Intoned the great Mongo traditional hymns
590   Which were taken up by all the different groups
       From all directions came wonderful ululations
       The crowds of dancers and singers shouted in praise of their Creator
       Their Ancestors, their Saviour, the Patriarch Ilele and his wife
       "Today is a great day in Mongo history
595   Today is the day of redemption and rebirth."
       Troubadours walked about the compound
       Singing, chanting spontaneous poems
       Elders and counsellors passed one by one before Lianja
       They bowed their heads before him
600   They talked to him with respect and softness
       The griots of different tribes and races narrated
       Stories and fables of ancient times
       Some even told about the wrestling match between Ilele and Mbombe
       They recounted how Ilele met her
605   How they married and came to Nkuma
       But they did not say how Ilele had died
       For the time was not ripe
       And they did not want to provoke Lianja's anger
       The wise narrators knew that Ilelangonda's death
610   Would create a bleak shadow in Lianja's mind
       It would disturb him so much

That he would not hesitate to revenge
They knew they would find a better way
To tell him the truth
615 It was prophesied that Lianja
Would unite all the tribes and races
But how would he reconcile
Two tribes which had always been enemies?
Nobody could see and believe the full truth of this prophecy
620 At that time, mankind's knowledge
About the Spirits' vision was very limited
They forgot that Lianja was both a spirit and a human being
In fact, *Ngiambe* would not have sent a mere mortal
For such a difficult task
625 *Ngiambe* the Creator, whose wisdom surpasses infinity
He who has existed, exists and will exist
Knows the shortcomings of humankind
Ngiambe knows how weak, selfish and corrupt His people are
They always speak of their own achievements, wealth and fantasies
630 Mankind is ignorant of the cycle of time as divided by *Ngiambe*
He created one cycle that He named earth
Where different creatures and humankind live and procreate
It is divided into days, nights and different seasons
In it, there is suffering, misery, death
635 Life, wealth, good and bad
Death takes away everything in this cycle
Then there is the cycle in which Himself *Ngiambe*
The Ancestors and Spirits live
This time cycle is endless
640 Those who dwell in it have external life
The two divisions have never met
Nor shall they ever met
For his part, Lianja had no doubt that he was sent by *Ngiambe*
To fulfil the most difficult task on earth
645 He did not care about people's doubts whatsoever!
He was well enough initiated to understand
Human beings' errors, thoughts, attitudes
He knew that mankind is often carried away by emotion
In the compound of his mother
650 The great celebrations continued
Their singing and chanting celebrated the historic day
The home of the Ancestors vibrated with the sounds of drums and trumpets
The joy of the living echoed

Into the fragile world of *Ngiambe's* creatures
655 If the day and the world were talkative and boastful like human beings
They would have chosen to narrate these events themselves
They, being the actual eye witnesses
Would have given no chance
To any griot to recount
660 What they had seen with their own eyes
Lianja and his sister Nsongo were watching
With keen interest the dances of the human beings
For them, it was the first time
They had seen creatures who looked like them
665 They marvelled at being born into a people
Who could dance and sing so well
Praise *Ngiambe* the Almighty
And eulogize all the Ancestors and the Spirits
Their voices were sunk in the oceans
670 Lakes of wild and noisy dancing and feasting
Some guest kings fell into a reverie and heard nothing more
Others dozed and dreamt about the past
Some were listening to a piece of quiet music
Played by a band of blind musicians
675 Softly the blind chanted: "Thank you Lianja, you're born today
You who are the chosen of all creatures on earth and heavens
Your name shall be exalted in songs, chants and poems
You have come into our midst so that
Our women may give birth to new progeny
680 You have brought light
To the ethnic groups and tribes of the earth
They shall all radiate with new fires of life
They shall make immortal your name
And that of our Ancestral Forefathers
685 They will sing songs to praise the one
Who reigns above every thing
Thank you Lianja, you have come
To plant the seeds of *Ngiambe's* vision
So that whoever will abide by it
690 Shall enjoy eternal life
Some brothers and sisters on this earth cosmos are carried away
Intoxicated by their own will
Filled with ill thoughts about their fellow man
Hating the earth *Ngiambe* so benevolently created for them
695 Thank you Lianja for being born among us

Because you will correct all these evils and mistakes."
The representatives of the evil spirits watched from afar
These delirious celebrations
They feared the new-born boy would see them
700 And curse them and bind them in trees
They should not have been there, for nobody had invited them
Though Lianja had seen them and monitored all their movements
He did not chase them away
Because he did not want to spoil the celebration
705 After all, he had come to fight a good fight against them
Who had been terrorizing *Ngiambe's* creatures on earth
After some hours, the singers and dancers took a rest
They drank, ate and refreshed themselves with traditional beer
The whole compound fell into silence when food was served
710 And Lianja had an opportunity to talk again to his mother:
"Mother, why do you not want to tell me where my father is?"
"Son," Mbombe replied, "once upon a time, your father went fishing
His boat was blown by a terrible storm
It sank and he died in the river."
715 Lianja did not believe what she told him
And insisted that the truth be told to him
"Mother, tell me the truth, where has my father gone?
Please, for the sake of your love for him, Nsongo and me
Tell us exactly where our father has gone?"
720 Mbombe, despite Lianja's plea, continued to tell him lies
Nobody knew why she continued to lie to her child
Such behaviour is uncommon among the Mongo
For whom the punishment for lying is beating and hanging
Some women shouted: "This woman, this Mbombe should be beaten to death
725 What kind of creature is she?
How can one tell lies to her own children?
Mbombe was afraid to tell the truth about her husband's death
Because she felt she was the person who had caused it
Had not Ilele died because of Mbombe's greed for rare fruits?
730 Was she the first woman to be pregnant in the whole of Mongoland?
Why did other men whose wives were pregnant not die
Why were they not killed by the Sau-Sau
Surely, the hero had not come to kill or destroy
But to give new dimensions to life and shape mankind's destiny
735 So Mbombe was afraid for no reason
Lianja finally realized that his mother was hiding something

He became very angry but could not do anything to her
She was the mother, the one who had given him birth only a few hours before
What then could Lianja do to discover
740 The truth about his father
On the basis of what his mother had told him
He called all the tortoises of the earth
And instructed them thus:
"You tortoises of the universe
745 Go into the water and meet with the aquatic creatures
Ask them where my father is
If you find him alive, bring him here
Tell him Nsongo and I have been born and are waiting to see him here
If he really died in water, take his skeleton and bring it
750 This command is of importance to all mankind
Go first to those aquatic creatures
Who dwell near our homes
If you do not find him there
Then set out into deep waters in search of him
755 Whatever happens
Be sure to fulfil this important mission."
As the tortoises left the villages of human beings
Lianja waited, hoping to hear shortly from them
Chief Tortoise, proud of serving the hero just-born
760 Led the concourse of tortoises
They searched everywhere in the rivers, lakes and oceans
Chief Tortoise's voice could be heard giving orders:
"Go deeper to the remotest area:
See first for yourselves if he is there
765 Then ask if you do not see him."
When they searched and did not find him
They all met at the shore
After the meeting at the shore, Chief Tortoise said:
"Let us go back again into water
770 This time, it is I who shall go ahead of every one
I shall interrogate all the aquatic animals and plants
If I see Patriarch Ilele, I shall summon you to join me."
Chief Tortoise went ahead·accompanied by five bodyguards
The other tortoises doubted
775 That the Patriarch had died in the river
As they were waiting on the shore
Chief Tortoise and his body guards came back

They went to Nkuma singing: "Elder brother Lianja
You have been told a lie by your own mother
780 Your father did not die in the water, while fishing in his boat
We have searched even the remotest parts of the rivers
But not a bone of his is there
Brother, they have cheated you
Your father is not in the rivers."
785 Lianja went again and approached his mother:
"Mother, you are deceiving yourself by telling me lies
I must know the truth about my father's death at all costs
No one but you should tell me how he died
Mbombe did not reply immediately
790 She kept silent for some minutes
Then she said: "Your father died while cutting a tree
The tree was so big that when it fell, it crushed him
He died, but his remains have never been found until this day
The tree killed him and buried also his crushed body."
795 After Mbombe had told Lianja this story
All the dwellers of the forests were called by the new-born hero
They were told to look for the bones and the skull of the Patriarch
Whoever would find them, would be given a reward
Chief Tortoise and the tortoises were again asked
800 To join the forest dwellers in search of the skull
First of all, the trees were interrogated
Then a tree was cut to see if a tortoise could escape
The tree did not fall on him nor did it crush him
The hunters concluded that a tree
805 Could not have killed the wise and intelligent Patriarch
"Brother Lianja, another lie, a dirty one
No tree could fall on the Patriarch and kill him instantly
We have cut the "bulumbu" tree and a tortoise was under it
When it fell, it did not kill the tortoise
810 It feared that it would drink blood
Brother Lianja, trees hate to drink human blood."

The Truth is Revealed

Lianja now changed his attitude to Mbombe, his mother
He also changed the tone of his voice
When he again addressed his mother about Ilelangonda
815 He carefully selected his words:

97

"Though I am your son, mother
I am able to make bad things happen to you
This time, if you tell me again a dirty lie
I shall cut off your head and make a cup of your skull
820 I shall cast your shadow from the cosmos of the Mongo Ancestors
You are embarrassing me, for you are behaving like a fool
You should know better the Mongo people and their traditions
I have only one desire:
To know the whereabouts of my father
825 From now on you shall not move
I shall free you only when you tell me what happened to my father
I am going to make a charm
If you smell it and tell me lies
Your life will come to an end
830 And your body will be reduced to ash."
Lianja lit a fire where he was with his mother
As he burnt the charm
He uttered the words:
Ngiambe the Creator, you made this earth as round as a globe
835 You created us to dwell in it and control it
You never wanted us to lie or kill
Whoever killed my father shall perish
And whoever gives false witness about his murder
Shall also perish
840 Anybody who knows the truth about this issue
Should be led by you to reveal it to me
This flame, Father *Ngiambe*, symbolises the truth."
The light opened Mbombe's thoughts and soul
It cleansed and purified her soul
845 She wept and confessed her sin to her child
Her shame made her kneel down before her son
She felt she had become a new creature
Suddenly, she had courage and started to speak:
"Lianja my son, forgive me for I have lied to you
850 You Ancestors, please do not curse me
I have lied to my child
Ngiambe, you who hears and sees every thing
Have mercy on me
I shall never again tell a lie
855 Lianja my son, hear now the truth:
"I sent your father to go and pluck some *nsafu* for me

When he climbed the Sau-Sau's sacred *nsafu* tree
The Sau-Sau and the Fete-Fete came with their birds
The hawk chopped his two eyes
60 His magic bell fell down
A female hawk broke his head
He fell to the ground
The Sau-Sau cut his body into small pieces
Then they wrapped it in wild leaves and sent it to us
65 It was horrible, very horrible my son
Your father died an awful death caused by the Sau-Sau!"
She wept, wept, wept and wept
Lianja consoled her and took her to her room
He also became very sad
70 He could not imagine how neighbours could do such an awful thing
He knew that, had he been there, his father would not have died
After much thought, he decided to send a messenger
To Chief Sau-Sau to convey the following message
"Know it, Oh! murderer
75 Your punishment for the murder of my father is to come
My father's blood was shed under a tree of wild fruits
Oh! murderer do you know who created that tree?
The crimes you have always committed
Have made you the greatest criminal of this land
80 You deserve a very severe punishment
I have come to show you the way you should follow
I have come to teach you how to behave
I have come to stop you from committing crimes
Great people are not ones who cause terror
85 Do you know how many great clans and tribes have crumbled
Through their own instigation?
Your spears and knives are sharp and your behaviour rude
Your killed my father and cut him into small pieces
You captured young Mongo girls and raped them!
90 What a crime!
The evil spirits and you share responsibility for the crimes
I, Lianja son of Ilele, just born some hours ago
I am the narrow end of a pin
You Chief Sau-Sau and your people have been very wild
95 You have been declaring war on your neighbours
Today, is born the one who will stop war for ever."
No Mongo was able to understand Lianja's boldness!

How could he dare provoke the most fearful warrior, Chief Sau-Sau!
Nobody doubted that because of Lianja's boldness
900   War between the Mongo and the Sau-Sau would soon break out
The living Mongo and the Sau-Sau did not realise
Lianja was a different creature sent by *Ngiambe*
He was part human being, part spirit
Though an infant, he was not an ordinary one
905   No human being on this earth or in the underearth cosmos could defeat him
He was a supernatural being, possessing great powers
For him, it would take a matter of seconds to kill his father's murderers
Take their land and make slaves of the survivors
He, Lianja, did not possess only supernatural powers
910   He also possessed natural strength, boldness and intelligence
He was very generous, but could also get annoyed,
Lianja decided to punish the Sau-Sau
He suddenly rang his magic bell and shouted:
"You monkeys, climb up all the trees in the Sau-Sau forests
915   Eat all the ripe fruit and throw away the green ones
You elephants, leave your creeks
Uproot all the Sau-Sau trees and eat all the roots
You boars under the moon, go into the Sau-Sau cassava plantations
Devastate all the fields and make the land a desert
920   You birds of the cosmos, use your wings, help the monkeys
Join with them, eat all the green leaves in the Sau-Sau fields
You rivers, lakes and oceans, dry up
May the aquatic creatures you bear die."
This is how Sau-Sauland was transformed into a living hell
925   By the Mongo hero Lianja
It became the residing place of all the evil forces
War between the Mongo and the Sau-Sau was declared
The Sau-Sau were very bitter against the Mongo
Chief Sau-Sau felt very offended by the infant Lianja
930   How can the Sau-Sau starve and die of hunger because of Lianja?
Who was he after all?
A useless infant without a father!
Chief Sau-Sau said: "This is the way fatherless children behave
They have nobody to educate them on matters concerning the world
935   I shall teach a lesson to the good-for-nothing Mongo boy
How can an infant challenge Chief Sau-Sau
Who among the Sau-Sau can argue with an infant?

Who among the Sau-Sau can talk the language of infants?
Let me go there, I shall kill that boy
'40   Crush him like an ant."
But it was not easy to crush Lianja
Although he was only an infant
Chief Sau-Sau and his people were deceiving themselves
Though they had been punished by Lianja
'45   Their barbarism and hooliganism did not stop at all
Dialogue between the Sau-Sau and the Mongo was not possible
The Sau-Sau were not ready to negotiate with an infant
So the only option left was war
The most powerful group would subjugate the other
'50   Until then, the Sau-Sau had been the most powerful
For them, no preparation for war against the Mongo was needed
They had always defeated them without any difficulty
They were simply waiting for Chief Sau-Sau to name the day and time
Lianja, on his side, trained his warriors seriously
'55   The Spirits called him to their cosmos
Where he spent three days and three nights
During which new powers and strengths were granted to him
He also learned new sophisticated war techniques
After three days in the cosmos of the Spirits
'60   Lianja ordered his warriors to retire into the Mongo forest
There the Ancestral Spirits visited them every day
Anointed them with magic oil
And infused them with new powers
When they had mastered the new war techniques
'65   They went back to Nkuma
No warrior was permitted to sleep with his wife
They all had to spend the nights together
The oracle had warned them not to be with a woman before war
For according to Mongo tradition
'70   Any warrior, hunter, fisherman or griot who indulged in sexual activity
Before the task ahead of him
Would not be blessed by the Ancestors and the Spirits
One day before the war, Lianja retired into the forest to meditate
During his meditation, he had a visitation
'75   He saw a spirit approaching him and talking to him:
"The war you are going to fight will open wider
The wounds of enmity between the Mongo and the Sau-Sau
The Mongo will win, the Sau-Sau will be killed

Their own crimes will sentence them to death
980 New life will be brought to them and their children
All the homes of the Mongo and the Sau-Sau will celebrate
The joys of brotherhood and neighbourliness
Go back, assemble your warriors and get ready
Tomorrow at midnight, your warriors
985 Will surround the whole of Sau-Sauland
Start attacking from the South
Then the East, then the North and West
Push all the Sau-Sau to the centre of the battlefield
Then finish them
990 You will be told what to do next and how to proceed."
Lianja went back to Nkuma and met with his warriors
After meeting all the warriors
He met with the best commanders
He explained to the strategists
995 The plan the Spirit had told him
The commanders and the strategists agreed with the Spirit's plan
In the evening of the same day, Lianja sent a second messenger
To warn Chief Sau-Sau of the impending Mongo attack
But Chief Sau-Sau did not heed the message
1000 He was certain of victory over the Mongo
There was no need for him to go into the battle-field with his warriors
He knew he possessed the herb of immortality
Given to him by the evil spirits
He knew, as usual, the evil spirits would fight for him
1005 His body was full of many magic herbs
Donated by the evil spirits
Apparently, the Sau-Sau were always ready for war
The night came when the two enemies
Had to meet face to face
1010 Mongo warriors armed themselves with poisonous spears and traditiona
guns
When they had positioned themselves at the most strategic places
The commander-in-chief blew a whistle that was heard by all
A Mongo medicine woman burst into Chief Sau-Sau's town shouting:
"You Chief Sau-Sau, assemble all your people
1015 Listen to these my words of wisdom:
Since your land has constantly been flooded with human blood
We have come to fight and conquer you
You wicked Sau-Sau and your dirty monsters, the evil spirits

Your soldiers will die, for they are cowards
020 Who only fight with the power of witchcraft
Such cowardly war techniques breach the rules of war
To kill an enemy, one needs strategies and intelligence, not witchcraft
Besides, all your soldiers are worn out retired people
We will wipe them out in no time
025 Get ready, we are here to kill without mercy!"
Chief Sau-Sau did not hear the words
Of the Mongo medicine woman
For he was deep asleep with his third wife
Whenever Chief Sau-Sau was drunk
030 He preferred to sleep with his third wife
The warriors and councillors came out of their houses
Nobody had the authority to reply to the challenge
Uttered by the medicine woman
Tradition allowed only Chief Sau-Sau
035 To make decisions about the security of the land
So they all waited for him to be awakened
No sooner had the Sau-Sau warriors and councillors
Started to discuss what strategies to adopt
Than the Mongo launched their attack
040 Spearheaded by the best trained and valiant young soldiers
Within less than an hour, they had conquered half of Sau-Sau territory
Set on fire their houses
And decimated every creature in the villages
The Sau-Sau were surprised
045 Those who survived quickly got organised
Men, women and children took spears and guns to defend themselves
The Mongo army, very cautious
Proceeded to divide itself into sections
As advised by the Spirit during his visitation
050 The best trained young warriors
Were followed by two wings
Which had encircled the territory
Preventing the Sau-Sau from escaping
Nsongo, Lianja's sister joined the third wing, led by General Kutu
055 Those warriors stationed in the eastern part of Sau-Sauland
Intensified their attacks
They pushed the Sau-Sau towards the centre of the battle field
Those who occupied the northern areas
Most of them experienced young female warriors

103

1060   Also attacked fiercely
Those who hid in forests and valleys advanced from West and South
Proceeding towards the centre
They all met at the capital city of Sau-Sauland
Where Chief Sau-Sau's women and children were sleeping
1065   After they had encircled Chief Sau-Sau's city and his own house
They made a temporary stop
And made instant communication with Lianja
Who instructed them to wait
Before attacking the capital city
1070   For he was on his way to the battlefield
Chief Sau-Sau, who was still asleep
Heard the commotion as though in a dream
His third wife woke him up
As he peeped through the door
1075   He saw a regiment of soldiers surrounding his house
He rushed to take one of his poisonous spears
As Chief Sau-Sau was preparing to attack the warriors around his house
He heard Lianja's voice at the door:
"You old rogue
1080   You have long claimed superiority over Mongo people
Today you must bow down to death
Like all the creatures you have killed
Never shall you challenge the truth of humanity
Sau-Sau, your country is a swarm of crime
1085   I have come to destroy your empire of evil
Unfold the palm-tree like a fig-tree
May your sisters and mine look at one another, woman to woman?
Can we meet face to face, like man to man?
Get ready to die, Oh! murderer of all times."
1090   These words uttered by Lianja in an authoritative voice
Troubled the Chief Sau-Sau
From all the sides of the Mongo regiments
Emerged great songs of war
Which broke the boundaries of the Sau-Sau horizons
1095   They filled the wide expanse of the Sau-Sau territory with fear
At that time, the Mongo were in control
They tore the garments off the Sau-Sau's diabolic forces
By their songs and the might of their number
They rose from the mist and scattered all over the capital city
1100   Invoking the sacred names of *Ngiambe*, the Ancestors and the Spirits

All of them hailed the trembling quietness of the morning
Chief Sau-Sau, who still was in his bedroom
Replied thus to Lianja's challenge:
"Lianja you are an infant
105   You did not exist when I killed your father
Before your father, do you know how many Mongo people
I personally had slaughtered?
Do you mean you are stronger than your Forefathers
Whose blood I drank?
110   No warrior on earth has ever defeated the Sau-Sau people
Your parents and relatives should have warned you
They should have told you the name of the one
Who is more powerful on this earth
Do not go away, let me come and smash your skull."
115   As Chief Sau-Sau came out of his house
Lianja shook his magic bell
Like a dry leaf, one of Lianja's spears
That had been sent to the cosmos of the Ancestors
Descended swiftly from the clouds
120   It did not follow a straight forward direction
It first took a left, then right turn
Then settled itself smoothly near the hero's legs
Even those Sau-Sau warriors who saw it
Conceded that it was beautifully wrought
125   It had no crack on it and was sharp and light
Nobody had ever possessed such a weapon
Lianja pulled out his magic bell
And gave it to Nsongo, who was standing near him
Suddenly, Chief Sau-Sau fiercely threw the first spear at Lianja
130   Then a second, a third and fourth
But none of them could touch Lianja
Who remained calm and immobile
He frowned at the unskilful warrior
Then braced his muscles to gain momentum
135   With intelligence and skill
He threw the spear which had descended from the clouds
It whistled as it flew in the air
Running faster than a star in the sky
Obediently, it took the direction dictated to it by the hero
140   It went, went and went until it sank into Chief Sau-Sau's heart
It pierced the heart

Traversed the stomach and the liver
It broke all the ribs from both sides; left and right
Chief Sau-Sau died
1145 Killed by Lianja
Spurts of blood erupted from both sides of his broken ribs
And bubbles of foam invaded the mouth of the chief terrorist
Lianja went nearer and peered at him
He saw the rough seeds of death
1150 He saw the roots of pain
Turning the evil Chief lifeless
Blood leaving the dead body
To form a pool to cleanse the Chief's last stains
Tears dried on Chief Sau-Sau's changing face
1155 Which looked black and wrinkled with the pain of death
Nsongo, the hero's sister wept
Not with sadness at Chief Sau-Sau's murder
But with the shock she felt in her heart as a girl
Lianja then retreated to a quiet place
1160 Where his sister followed him
As they sat together on a large stone
Nsongo suddenly saw Lianja's eyes light up
Like a fierce thunderbolt, a voice came from the skies
Piercing through the minds of the warriors
1165 The clouds opened widely their hands to the universe
The rivers and oceans became perfectly happy
The soil that imbibed the dead warriors' blood
Was washed up by rains of blessing
The bad blood that existed between the two peoples
1170 Was washed away
Giving way to new blood of peace, brotherhood and love
The voice shouted happily the name of Lianja:
"Lianja, Lianja, son of Spirits, we appreciate your action
For such is the beginning of your mission on earth
1175 That is why you have been born in a world of imperfection
The whole mankind has suffered the sadness of its crime
The hooliganism of the Sau-Sau has spilled blood in the region
The children of Mongoland have been killed by the Sau-Sau
The nourishment of their lives has been curtailed by the Sau-Sau crimes
1180 Your hand will feed both peoples
Go back, take your magic powder
Infuse it in the nostrils of the dead

Resurrect them all and depart to the promised land."
As the voice addressing Lianja and Nsongo ceased
1185   She wept for the dead brothers and sisters:
"Lianja my brother
Why have you killed your brothers?
Lianja my brother
Although they killed our father
1190   We must love the Sau-Sau and the Fete-Fete
Lianja my brother, please do what the voice has commanded you,"
Lianja went back to the battle field
Took his magic powder and infused it in the dead warriors' nostrils
When all the dead, Sau-Sau and Mongo, had come back to life
1195   And regained their senses
Lianja cut the tree of calamity and in its place
Planted a young tree of peace and reconciliation

The Journey to the Promised Land

After the tree of reconciliation had been planted
A big celebration was held
1200   Then it was time for Lianja to lead the two tribes to the new land
Before their departure
Lianja addressed the people thus:
"Brothers and sisters
The power of humankind must succumb to that of *Ngiambe*
1205   It is this truth that has always surpassed all truths
The evil spirits possess a blade
Among the living here on earth
Their power always strikes against the righteous
It threatens the righteous who obey the truth of *Ngiambe*
1210   We on earth should learn to discern his truth
From the evil one
And avoid involvement in diabolic and evil activities
Those who carry the powers of the devil
Will have to pay for it
1215   Let the forces of the Spirits overwhelm those of the evil ones
Let us try to practise this
On our long journey to the new land
If we here on earth live on what *Ngiambe* has given us
We will distinguish ourselves from beasts

1220	There never will be war, hatred, jealousy or envy
	If it was only power that decided the might of a land
	Then the most powerful beasts would be the rulers of all lands
	Powerful as our elephants are
	They only feed on soft grass
1225	Though they can use their power
	To kill the small animals and eat them
	These huge animals are conscious of their strength
	But they make good friends with all creatures
	We also make friends with whoever
1230	We shall conquer en route to the promised land
	Get ready for we are beginning a long journey
	I, Lianja, and my sister Nsongo, will lead you
	Until we shall reach the great land
	We shall drink water from the river of life
1235	Nobody will stop us on our way
	We shall defend ourselves
	Against any enemy who will dare attack us
	Let us take the tatoos of our race
	Let us cover our bodies with adornments
1240	Let us arm ourselves with spears and necklaces
	May *Ngiambe* and the Ancestral Forefathers protect our lives
	Let us wake up and go,"
	After Lianja had spoken to the united race in these terms
	The elders decided on a new tribal mark:
1245	Two oblique lines on the face for men
	Three small juxtaposed lines on the body for women
	Other stamps of identification were branded on both men and women
	Lianja chose the ornaments and weapons that they would take with them
	Necklaces, pearls, and bangles of copper, iron and brass
1250	Adorned the ankles and wrists
	Daggers across the back, and in their hands, they carried shields
	They were also armed
	With bows, arrows, spears, javelins and machetes
	Then there was a special necklace chosen by Lianja
1255	That they all wore around their necks
	So adorned, the new race broke into a triumphant song
	As the sun rose and began to cast light on the earth
	They all joined in the great sound and set off to the unknown land
	Many curious eyes from the cosmos of the Ancestors followed them
1260	Young and beautiful female Spirits admired and revelled in their singing

The song of pride was repeated in chorus by women and children:
"Through mountains, valleys, hills and forests, we shall pass
We shall march without wearing out our legs
Lianja, our leader, will take us to the new land of our Ancestors
1265   Where we shall drink the water of life
Where a new generation shall be born
Where our race shall be perpetuated for ever."
Through a lonely landscape, the caravan passed
Their number increased with new recruits
1270   Who joined in the journey to the new land
The sun was at the point of death
Sliding over the horizon
The shadows of the forest trees creeping eastward
The lights went on at dusk throwing their green shadows
1275   Like a huge and large veil on darkened peaks
Fire appeared like a gigantic swarm of fireflies
Suddenly, like a thunder clap, music broke out from far
Voices of human beings were heard in that forest
People were living there
1280   They were celebrating, singing and dancing
The occasion was a wedding
On hearing the voices Lianja transformed himself into a small boy
Because his huge build would frighten
The peaceful singers and dancers
1285   He then approached the oldest of the group, asking:
"Who are you."
"We are musicians, this is our land
And we are rejoicing for a wedding
And you who are you?" replied Bofala the oldest musician
1290   "Do you know that Lianja is passing through this land?
How do you ask such a question?"
Responded one of the travellers
Lianja, then borrowed Bofala's zither and began to play
He played so well that he impressed the other musicians
1295   They decided to follow him
For more sweet melodies
All the families, all the clans
And the whole tribe of musicians left their homes
They joined the travellers on their journey to the new land
1300   After a while they reached an arid place
Where lived some funny creatures with shapeless bodies

Lianja urged his people to be alert
For he had anticipated hostility in that land
After they had crossed that region
1305 They saw a beautiful landscape
Baobab trees with rafter leaves created a beautiful scene
The leaves alternated with cassava fields
Maize plantations formed big furrows
The plants were very tall
1310 The travellers could not see beyond the field
As they proceeded, they saw mango trees
That consorted with orange trees
Palm trees, raising up their branches formed a shield
To protect all these village trees
1315 A dozen *kapokier* trees stood proud and tall
Birds nests built on the *kapokier* branches
Appeared to be floating in the skies
Avocado and coconut trees announced the beginning of human settlement
Over which flew innumerable sparrow-hawks
1320 Fishermen were living in that beautiful earth paradise
Whose huts had pointed thatched roofs
Suddenly, a bearded old man with one eye appeared
He greeted the passers-by
Lianja saluted him with respect and asked who he was
1325 The old one-eyed man answered: "I am the Chief of this village
The guarantor and protector of a tribe
Whose capital city is this village
My people have gone fishing and will come late at night
You all are invited to take a rest
1330 Palm-wine will be brought to you
Please sit and have something to quench your thirst
Your journey must have been so long that you walked day and night."
After palm-wine kegs had been circulated among the travellers
Lianja asked the ugly one-eyed man to take him to the nearest fishing ground
1335 Which turned out to be a river
What a blessing after several days' walk without refreshment!
The travellers drank water, took baths and washed their clothes
Then they went back to the fishermen's village
As they entered the village
1340 Some fishermen came to attack them
Despite the village Chief's kindness and desire not to fight
The whole tribe of fishermen, and even women, fought the travellers

But Lianja's troops, very experienced and many in number, killed all of them
And set their beautiful village ablaze
1345 Then with his magic powder
Lianja resurrected the dead among his own
And the fishermen too
And they all set off on their journey to the land of peace
They travelled endlessly, passing through forests, valleys and mountains
1350 One day, during the dry season, standing on an ant-hill
Lianja saw on the other side of the mountain
A wisp clinging to a tree like a light scarf
That signified a village inhabited only by single women
It was lifeless, useless and hot as a tomb
1355 Glowing powerful lights illuminated some of the women
Who were busy pounding maize and cassava
A young woman who was in her thirties
Was humming nonchalantly a languid stanza
That her comrades repeated with faith
1360 She did not seem to worry about her spinsterhood
She appeared to be the prettiest woman
Her face radiating with beauty
Her legs and arms very clean
Anointed with *kaolin* ointment
1365 Her gaze and body movements followed
The rhythm of the pestles
So elated she was, she sang with the other old spinsters:
"We are alone but not lonely,
Our love for man was weakened by his behaviour
1370 Though our wombs have never conceived
Humankind has never cursed us
And our race shall never perish
For we respect the sacred laws of heaven
Does our spinsterhood violate the boundaries of creation?
1375 We are armed with our respect and freedom
We do not mean to annihilate humankind
By not giving birth to children
One day the sun will nourish the growth of our spinster race
And a great male voice shall halt our condition
1380 Our life shall begin from where that of man and woman together begins
We shall rise in greatness
Until all the Ancestral powers will be restored on us
We shall live, we shall not perish."

As they were singing these words
1385 Lianja sat dejectedly
His head resting on his two bare hands
He shouted out against their lamentation:
"Your status as spinsters does not mean
The annihilation of humankind
1390 No one should forget to hail *Ngiambe's* will
Mankind must, according to His will
Multiply through women and men
You should ask the Creator to open His gifts for you
So you can possess the great powers of life with men
1395 Life has listened, and today is your day for breaking through
Your harsh voices have stopped the hurricane
That would halt creation
Often times juicy fruits grow and rot on the trees
While people go hungry and starve to death
1400 Even the Spirits return thanks to *Ngiambe*
For their capability of procreation
Your barren days shall soon carry the joy of nights."
As the male travellers entered the village with Lianja
They sauntered with pride
1405 The spinsters welcomed them
And led them to the village public place
With naked bosoms, the spinsters huddled around the men
Old and mature women, they shouted:
"We have now got husbands
1410 Let us try our luck and celebrate the goodwill of *Ngiambe*, the Creator."
The other female travellers helped to cook food
And organise the marriage banquet
After they all had eaten, danced and drunk
Lianja planted an arrow on the tomb of the Queen spinster
1415 As a token of dowry for the new marriages
After the ceremony, he blessed each couple and they all thanked *Ngiambe*
The following day, the roosters of the village crowed very late in the morning
To awake the new couples
Having given them time to enjoy their first night together
1420 When everybody had awoken
The journey started again, heading southward
As they journeyed, the caravan was joined by various tribes:
Blacksmiths, beer brewers, palm-wine tapsters
Extracters of palm-oil, tailors, farmers, sculptors,

1425   Hunters, painters, builders, architects, runners and divers
All were happy to go to the new land of survival
Their favourite triumphant anthem went thus:
"Through mountains, valleys and hills
We shall pass without tiring
1430   Lianja is our leader
He will lead us to the extremes of the earth cosmos
Every danger in the rivers, forests and valleys shall be overcome
We shall reach the land promised by *Ngiambe*
Where we shall live in peace
1435   Where our race, now merged as one will perpetuate."
The tropical sun burnt down hot and hard
Humidifying the air
And making it difficult to breathe
From afar they saw a hut
1440   Protected from heat and rain by a tangle of magic plants
Which communicated with the devil
The plants served as the ears and the eyes
Through which Yampunungu, a feared one-legged sorcerer, could hear and see
Everything everywhere
1445   He had all the magic and feared evil forces
No human being had ever stepped on the land of the one-legged man
Lianja and his people were the first human beings
To have the guts to provoke the old man
As he sat peacefully under the shadow of his hut
1450   Yampunungu looked cruel, unconquerable and wily
Leaning on a crutch, he could move as fast as a star
He crooned: "I am Yampunungu, the most feared conqueror
I have fought fierce wars and battles
I have remained invincible
1455   Countless are the enemies who have lost their lives to me
Strangers, what do you want of an experienced warrior?
Pass, continue your journey without disturbing the peaceful warrior."
Nsongo, the hero's sister, was very scared
She had never seen such a man before
1460   She whispered to Lianja "This lonely man is going to kill us
We must get out of this land
He claims to be a powerful warrior."
Lianja was not afraid because he knew he would trap the man easily
"Remain here, he said to his sister and his followers

1465 I shall catch him with craft. Watch the operation."
Lianja crept through the leaves towards the old warrior's hut
Where a big fire burned continuously as a symbol of powerful warriors
Lianja changed himself into a cricket, went through the open door
And waited for the warrior
1470 As Yampunungu entered the hut
He realised that a cunning stranger had gone in
The one-legged man walked out and went to sleep with the evil spirits
Knowing that Yampunungu had gone away
Lianja changed back into a human being
1475 He went to his people and transformed them into grass
Then they waited for Yampunungu near his hut
Yampunungu knew strangers were around waiting for him
Lianja transformed himself into a log of wood
He dropped himself on the ground for the warrior to get him
1480 But Yampunungu refused to touch that log of wood on the grass
Lianja became a boa, ran without fear in the woods
Climbed very tall trees and went around a grove of bamboos
He continued his race and met different herds of animals
Which had stopped here and there to bite some twigs
1485 A crackling of broken branches and the boa was in a ditch
Caught up in a very tricky running knot
Yampunungu ran after it with wide open eyes
He searched under the plants, his spear in hand
He threw a big stone to kill the snake hidden in the ditch
1490 When he noticed that it was not a real snake
He shouted: "Lianja, you are a mere child
Please note that I am Yampunungu, the eternal conqueror
I know you are not a real boa constrictor, if you are, become a worm."
Immediately, Lianja changed into a big worm
1495 Many other worms around him began to swarm in the forest
Although the boa changed into worm as he had ordered
The one-legged man did not try to catch it, knowing it was Lianja
"He and his people have been spying on me," sighed the old man
He left the boa alone and went to appear in another forest
1500 Lianja followed him there and became an antelope
In that savannah lived many herds of gazelle, oxen, wild cows,
Squirrels, wild rabbits, hamsters, beavers, anteaters and shrews
Yampunungu came quietly and saw the antelope
He had a feeling that it was not a genuine animal to hunt
1505 He then shouted: "I am Yampunungu the conqueror

114

I wonder what you are doing in this savannah if you are not a real animal!
If you are not a genuine animal, may worms eat you up."
Nothing happened to the animal
Which was looking at him timidly
1510 Yampunungu went back starving to his house
He had caught no animal
The following day, he went to inspect his traps
He was hungry for he had eaten no meat for two days
The savannah was quiet and a bird was singing
1515 A breeze from the south was caressing gently the soft dusty grass
The one-legged hunter said to himself:
"I am very hungry
Since that silly boy, Lianja, has been in my territory
I have had nothing to eat
1520 Why then should I leave an antelope to rot in this ditch
Why should one fear a small boy like Lianja and go hungry."
The wizard man took a rope and made some running knots
Leaned over the ditch, lashed the animal's head and legs together
Pulled the antelope out and put it down on the grass
1525 He waited some minutes before slaughtering his prey
As he pulled out his knife to cut the head of the antelope
Lianja emerged from the rotting animal
He got hold of the old man's only leg
Felled him and tied his hands
1530 This is how Yampunungu came to be the Mongo's slave
It was noon and the sun's beams spread their dazzles everywhere
The concourse of travellers peacefully went on their journey
They reached a pool full of fish
Which the female travellers started to scoop out
1535 The noise made by the women soon reached the owners of the pool
Who were all ogresses
They rushed there and started threatening the fisherwomen with death
"Who is scooping out Bofunga's pool?
Who allowed you to get fish from her pool?
1540 This is Bofunga's pool
We are going to kill all of you."
Nsongo retorted with the same arrogance:
"This pool belongs to *Ngiambe*, not to dirty ogresses
We shall continue to get fish from it
1545 We shall cook the fish and feed our children and husbands
Who are you to threaten us with such arrogance?"

With vexation, the ugly ogresses bustled out
They spat on the ground and in the water to frighten the fisherwomen
After they had spat to scare the people
1550 They stripped off their clothes to curse the Mongo
We are going to call our husbands
You will see the powers of the ogre warriors."
As they left the pool, Lianja assembled all the fisherwomen
"Take all your fish, let us go away
1555 There is no need to fight with monsters
Nobody would like to take monsters as slaves
Because no ogre has ever been useful to humankind
Despite their herculian power, ogres have always been cruel."
As Lianja and his people were preparing to leave the ogres' land
1560 They heard from far the ominous howling of a host of ogres
Who were running so fast that they reached the Mongo in two minutes
Lianja knew that fighting would not help his people
A giant *kapokier* tree appeared in front of the Nkundo hero
It had a lot of fruits and its trunk was very big
1565 Lianja invoked the Mongo Ancestors in these terms:
"Ancestors, Spirits
Please listen to my prayer
Shadow of shadows, force of forces
Eternal powers of the bush, mountain, valley and forest
1570 You who haunt rocks and trees in waters and forests
Oh supreme forces, do not abandon your faithful servants
Spirits of all times, may you lend me your ears!
May your powers be mine today for combating the evil forces
I shall serve you for ever without fail."
1575 As he finished invoking the Ancestors and the Spirits
He beat the trunk of the tree with his right hand
The lianas covering the tree from the top shook
The tree also shook and bowed its branches
The crowds huddled themselves under the tree of safety
1580 Lianja said: "Friends, climb the tree and sit on the branches."
He then beat again the trunk of the tree of safety
Suddenly, from the soil where the roots were,
The tree heaved and the people were thrown into the sky
When the ogres came, they saw nobody
1585 As they saw nobody at the pool, they looked around
As they were looking around, Lianja spat on them
Drops of saliva fell on them as a sign of a curse

Chief Bofunga looked up and saw Lianja with his people up in the sky
She sang "Look up, look up, brothers and sisters,
1590 Lianja and his people are seated on the branches
Let us cut the tree and capture them
We shall deal with them mercilessly
Let us climb this tree and cut all its branches
We shall kill the Mongo travellers without mercy."
1595 Lianja taunted them and teased them:
"You fools, go and die in the wilderness
May the whirlwinds transport your dead bodies to the arid lands."
These words from the traveller hero vexed the chief ogress
Who made a knot like a hoop and climbed the tree
1600 As she neared the branch Lianja was sitting on
The hero shook his magic bell and the ogress fell down and died
All the ogres and ogresses were enraged by their Chief's death
A group of elderly ogres made five hoops
Tied them around the tree and their bodies then started up the tree
1605 As they neared the branch on which Lianja was seated
The Nkundo hero cut the five hoops and they too died like their chief
The rest of the ogres decided to cut down the tree
Sharp axes, machetes and wood saws were brought
When the tree of safety was almost ready to fall
1610 Lianja shook his magic bell, struck it against the *kapokier*
And sang: "Tree of safety, recover
Heal your wounds and remain unhurt
Hold me and my people without failure
Remain safe and untouched
1615 The people of *Ngiambe* will never fail in the hands of evil ogres."
The tree, which was falling, straightened up again
It healed its wounds and remained unhurt
The ogres called upon their allies
Who flocked from every corner of the world
1620 They begun again to cut
They dug and uprooted it over days and nights
The tree quivered but did not fall down
Lianja caressed its trunk
The tree healed again its wounds and remained unhurt
1625 Tired, the monsters finally gave up
They understood that they could not defeat the Mongo hero
The travellers came down from the tree
And continued their journey safely

	At daybreak Lianja led the travellers to the South
1630	The sun spread its beams throughout the earth and skies
	The day was adorned with the reddish sunbeams of dawn
	Which lit the distant areas and opened the mind of the hero
	The caravan crossed a stream by means of a ford
	And reached a very hostile area afflicted by earthquakes, tornado's and cyclones
1635	Millions of birds were flying lightly as though chased by a hunter
	Lianja did not know that another group of ogres
	Was sharing the area with the natural disasters
	Armed to the teeth, they were hiding, waiting to capture the travellers
	In fact, these ogres were more ferocious than the first group
1640	And were angry at the defeat of their fellow ogres
	The hero and his people were tired of fighting
	But they had to defend themselves and find their way
	To the land of survival *Ngiambe* and the Ancestors had promised
	The proud ogres had already conspired with the hills, mountains and valleys
1645	To prevent the travellers from passing through their territory
	Lianja, after weighing all the strategies
	Planned to capture first their Chief
	The hero could see through his magic bell, hundreds of ogres
	With their odd physical forms jumping in the forest like monkeys
1650	Quaint shadows appeared at the peaks of trees
	The whole forest was in turmoil
	Lianja ordered his people to sit under a big baobab tree
	While he went to confront alone the multitude of powerful monsters
	The Chief, who was eating some ripe fruit with relish
1655	Was informed of an arrogant stranger in their midst
	The ogre was very heavy for he had eaten a lot of fruit
	Lianja knew it would be easier to capture the glutton beast
	Once he had eaten his fill of fruit
	Thousands of ogres were employed to pluck apples for the chief ogre
1660	And bring them to him without eating even one
	He would lie down on the grass every evening
	And open wide his huge mouth
	While other ogres threw apples into it
	He would gulp them down with incredible talent
1665	And so Lianja transformed himself into a very ripe, juicy apple
	And appeared on the tree under which chief ogre was seated
	The ogre's wife saw the apple, plucked it and gave it to him
	As he put it to his mouth, a magician ogre held back the chief ogre's righthand

But chief ogre, too greedy, had quickly swallowed the juicy apple
1670 As soon as he swallowed it, he pulled a weary face
Lianja went straight into the ogre's stomach
And settled comfortably in the centre
He shook the beast's stomach with force
Cut up the intestines and chopped into pieces the chief ogre's heart
1675 Foam bubbled from his mouth
Big drops of sweat fell from his chest and face
Lianja twisted the ogre's pancreas
And blood came through the mouth
He detached the lungs, and let them fall to the ground
1680 Where jackals pounced on them and ate them all
Chief ogre died and thereafter Lianja easily killed all the ogres
Lianja was proud he had acted faster than the ogres
Who were known to flee very fast
When confronted with danger
1685 With a great roar of songs and anthems, the Mongo set off again
On their journey to the new land
The memory of the fight against the ogres won them new courage
They became a great nation
Lianja, their hero, had spared them many tragedies
1690 Indeed, the Ancestors and Spirits had great respect for them
As a people who had sworn to reach the land of survival at any cost
They passed through large settlements of evil people
Who had earned fame through murder and outrageous acts
By the mysterious power of his mind
1695 Lianja put them into a deep sleep for one week
After the travellers had passed the evil people's settlements,
Lianja brought rain, floods and thunders on that land for three weeks
Finally the Mongo reached the most dangerous area
Lights as bright as sunbeams suddenly appeared above Lianja's head
1700 "Nsongo my sister, look up, what is that above my head?" asked the hero
At the same time Nsongo also was illuminated from head to toe
"Lianja my brother, why am I white as snow?
What has happened to my black skin?" replied Nsongo
Lianja stopped and looked up a palm tree
1705 Invaded by a gigantic snake, as big as the mouth of a sky
This enormous snake was called Master Indombe
And it was as dreaded as the plague
When the Nkundo hero saw it, he saluted it saying:
"Patriarch Indombe, I know we are in your most beautiful land

119

1710	Please come down and welcome us as your friends
	We need something to drink for we are thirsty
	Our journey has been very long and tiring."
	Indombe, with his flexible head full of thorns
	Coiled his tail, and opened wide his mouth to say:
1715	"Foolish Mongo boy, aren't you vain?
	Master Indombe cannot go down to welcome his Mongo enemies
	If you have a problem, go and tell it to your mother and father
	Why do you think I must feed you hooligans?"
	Lianja, using flattering language, pleaded with him thus:
1720	"Indombe, King of Kings
	You rule over the forests, valleys, mountains and rivers
	Please come down and welcome your visitors from far lands
	Please Master Snake, show us your hospitality."
	But the words of flattery did not amuse the snake
1725	Who waved his head as if to bite the Mongo visitor:
	"Roguish, vile and indisciplined child." Indombe roared
	"Stupid boy, did your father and mother send you to abuse me?
	How can you ask me to go down and welcome silly people? Do you
	know who you are talking to?
1730	Your boldness is without limits."
	The snake crept behind the main branch of the palm-tree
	And passed quietly through the palm leaves
	Black shadows from one branch to another escorted the King of Snake Kings
	Lianja stared at him, huge and lithe, and said:
1735	"Master Indombe, you have come down following my command!
	Did I not tell you you shall always obey the hero's command?
	I am going to fight and kill you
	Wait a minute, I am going to tell the sun to come back
	So that it will give me light until I kill you."
1740	It was late in the evening,
	The cosmos was already dark after a beautiful sunset
	An evening wind was blowing from North to South
	And the Mountains were drowned in darkness
	Like a buffalo in a big river
1745	Earth and heavens were quiet
	Listening to Lianja's command: "Sun, come back
	Start again the day and take back your place in the sky
	Because I need light to fight and kill this deadly creature."
	The sun promptly obeyed the Mongo hero
1750	It took back its place and started shining in the East

Before the fight began, Indombe cursed Mongo people
"May Lianja's brothers and sisters be cursed by the devil
May Mongoland become so arid
That no crops will ever grow in it and no rain shall fall
1755 May the beasts of this forest tear Lianja into pieces
May this idiot boy's body become dust
For he has no respect for elders like Indombe."
After the dreadful snake had cursed Lianja and his people
He flew and landed on Lianja's shoulders
1760 Encircling his neck in a grip so tight
That Lianja almost collapsed
The weight of the snake's head alone was three times that of the hero
But in spite of all this
The Mongo hero remained confident and sturdy
1765 Indombe breathed with pride, as though victory was already his
He darted out his perfidious tongue to frighten Lianja
But Lianja stood upright, his feet fixed solidly on the ground
And refused to be defeated by the devil's servant
Lianja pretended to whine and plead to be set free
1770 Grumbled and clenched his teeth
While secretly, he took his magic bell and put it on his right shoulder
Without knowing, the Master-Snake raised himself
And lay his big and heavy head on it
Under the weight of the snake
1775 The heros body sank deep into the ground
But it neither shook, nor did it sway from side to side
Lianja uttered the following words, heard by the attendant travellers:
"I am the victorious Lianja
I am the invincible Lianja
1780 The undried wood that cannot burn
I shall always act like a man."
He shook his bell, which rang weakly because of the weight of Indombe
Lianja took a deep breath and shouted
"Nsongo my sister, quickly give me my knife
1785 Now that all my strength has returned
Let the son of man and Spirits finish the devil's child."
Lianja took his sharp knife and thrust it into Indombe's mouth
Tore it into two and then smashed the stomach and the tail
With a stroke of his knife
1790 Lianja vanquished the gigantic last child of the demons
Ending domination by demons in that area

At Last, the Promised Land

After killing their last enemy
The travellers continued on the journey to the land of survival
To encourage the travellers, who were very exhausted
1795   Lianja started a refrain that was soon taken up by all:
"We shall find the land of survival
We shall remain victorious on our way to the land of survival."
Woody savannahs became scarce in the area
Tall trees prevented the travellers from seeing the horizon
1800   The vegetation became green, the weather cool
And a fresh breeze swept away the travellers' fatigue
The cool air renewed their bodies and minds
Refreshed their intelligence and souls
Opened their eyes and spirits
1805   Was the journey over? These signs, did they portray the land of life?
None of them knew, but Lianja did
He knew that the river of life was just around the corner
He saw millions of ferocious black ants
Moving in Indian file toward the river of life
1810   He also saw paths and forked roads
All of them leading to the river of life
Lianja became very cautious
He did not want to miss the way at the last minute
He asked the travellers to stop and take a rest
1815   While they ate and refreshed themselves
Lianja went to an isolated place to praise and glorify *Ngiambe*
After he had prayed, praised, glorified and worshipped *Ngiambe*
And after the travellers had eaten and drunk
Lianja assembled all the women, children and men
1820   When they were all seated on the green grass, Lianja said:
"Great, indeed very great, has been our journey for many years
Our long journey symbolizes the bond between us and *Ngiambe*, the Creator
The link between the Mongo and their Ancestors and the Spirits
Brothers and Sisters, here is our land as it was prophesied
1825   This land marks the end of years of sufferings, hatred and war
This land shall breed life in abundance
All the Mongo people shall follow the ancient paths of their Ancestors
We all here have witnessed the rebirth of the earth cosmos
No one shall plant again the seeds of hatred and jealousy
1830   You shall always safeguard the great truths of life

Here on the land of survival, all things and creatures shall dwell
You Mongo people shall control your own lives
And that of other creatures
You shall experience new life and new vision
1835   Our Ancestors and the Spirits see our world change every day
They are the proud eternal possessors of the true life and its meaning
Their spiritual powers surpass those of evil spirits and their servants
The Ancestors' powers came from *Ngiambe*, the moulder of this cosmos
They do not change with the whims of events in our life
1840   Instead, they eternally enrich the seeds of mankind's life
They teach us the great anthem our Forefathers sang in their lives
Ngiambe, the Ancestors and the Spirits threw the light of truth in our eyes
Today, they have made us find their great gift as promised
To us it was a dream but for them it was a reality
1845   My mother, my sister and I are returning where we came from
Giving you authority to sing eternally with the Ancestors and the Spirits
The anthem of love, peace and unity at our mammoth rivers of life
Where we are going, we shall wait for your triumphant coming
And shall accompany you with pride to your last eternal resting place
1850   At the centre of your life, should be the force of love and justice
Plant the seeds of these values in your minds and souls
And your conduct will shine with the light of righteousness
For we are the custodians of a loving and righteous force
That has moulded us and makes us move in the right direction
1855   You have received the power of life
That you will pass on to your children and the children of your children
You shall help them open their eyes
In a way that the cycle of procreation will be always celebrated
All your thoughts, minds, souls and voices must always remain together
1860   Your tradition will rest sacred
And will unveil the precints of Mongo culture
Ushering new ideas and new Mongo generations eager to grow
We are the children of *Ngiambe*, the Ancestors and the Spirits
This truth shall remain for ever the truth
1865   Those of this earth who do not have this truth in their hearts
Shall never never live in the land of survival."
As the Mongo hero spoke
Ngiambe, the Ancestors and the Spirits in the heavens
Opened wide their ears and eyes
1870   And endorsed these truths from the saviour hero
They showered wisdom in the minds of the Mongo people

And shed the light of truth in the numerous paths of their life
After Lianja had finished his last speech
He went with his sister and mother to a young palm tree
1875 He took his mother on his shoulder and his sister on his knees
They climbed the young palm-tree and disappeared in the clouds forever
Dismayed, the Mongo people decided to follow their hero
They cut tall trees and tied them together
But they could not reach the cosmos of the Spirits and the Ancestors
1880 Where Lianja, his sister and mother had gone to live
The trees broke and the Mongo were hurled far and wide
Wherever they landed, they built big villages and cities
And never again spoke Lianja's name
But Lianja is surely about to come back to Mongoland
1885 Because disease, murder and all names of evil are rampant again in Mongoland.

END

Notes on the text

1. Ngiambe can be translated into English as God, the Creator. The Mongo people believe that He is the Creator of all things, visible and invisible; The provider and the protector who cares for all His creatures.

2. Waku-Waku is the name of a wise intelligent and courageous Mongo ancestor. Because of his boldness, Waku-Waku was the spokesman of his community. A man full of initiative, he dedicated his life to his people. He was not a political leader as such but somebody who preached good conduct to avoid the disintegration of society. The name Waku-waku is still given today to those men in Mongo society who have wisdom and intelligence; those dedicated to their communities and who are willing to die for it.

3. *Bilima* is a Lingala word for spirit. *Bi* is used for plural so *Bilima* is the plural of *Elima*. I have decided to use a capital "s" for describing the good spirits who protect, but when written with a small *"s"*, it refers to the "devils", "bad spirits" who live in under-earth cosmos.

4. Iania Anzaka Bokulu Tondi is the name of the Spirit who appears in Mongoland to announce the hero's birth. It is believed that the spirits and Lianja himself are one and the same. In some versions of the epic, the hero is referred to as 'Iania' while in others he is called 'Lianja'.

5. Mama Isaso was an intelligent, wise and brave Mango woman who could stand and speak for her people with eloquence and wisdom. Her talents were also recognised by the Spirits and Ancestors. The name Isaso is given today to any Mongo female who shows courage and intelligence. It is a common name mainly among the Mongo of kutu, Omongo, Kiri and Mbadaka. (see the map of Zaire).

6. The Sau-Sau are imaginary tribe which are pitched against the Mongo in this epic. The Mongo represent God's people while the Sau-Sau, evil force is manifested and it claims equality with *Ngiambe* the Almighty.

7. Mongo people have developed a very interesting mode of communication through drums, rattles and many other musical instruments. Drums poetry is widespread among the Mongo and other Zairean groups.
   Waku-Waku's drumming in the text represents a spoken utterance in a way intelligible and understandable to Mongo listeners. Through it, the Mongo people are informed of the Spirit's appearance and are told to prepare themselves to welcome him.

8. Biongo is a Mongo ancestors who is believed to have been a very good leader. A democratic ruler who fears *Ngiambe* and communes with the Spirits. A leader loved by all Mongo people because of his political style. A respected and respectful chief who loves and cares. A man of wisdom,

intelligence and many other abilities. He is quoted even today as an example of good leadership.

9. As mentioned in the introductory notes, time in this epic text is not measured in terms of seconds, minutes or hours. Rather, is the importance of the event which counts. When the narrator says: many moons or a hundred years; he is speaking metaphorically.

"Many moons" is the nearest translation of "basanza mingi", which if translated as "many months" does not really capture the narrators meaning.

10. Those Mongo living in Imongo and Kiri have common village boundaries with the Botwa.

11. The devil or evil spirit.